IN CHARGE

A SWEETGUM MEADOWS ROMANCE
BOOK FIVE

IMANI PRICE

First Edition: October 2023

ISBN 978-1-960207-56-2 (ebook)
ISBN 978-1-960207-57-9 (paperback)

Published by Books to Hook Publishing, LLC.
www.BooksToHook.com

CONTENTS

CHAPTER ONE

$\mathcal{A}$mber leaves swirled in small whirlwinds, moving past Joanne's parked car. As she stepped out, they crunched beneath her leather boots. The door shut with a firm thud, followed by the chirp of the locking mechanism.

"It's around the corner down Mabel Lane. This one used to be a thrift store before the owner moved out of town," Mr. Jones said as he twisted a key into his convertible, locking his door. He waited as she caught up to him, then pocketed his free hand. Joanne could tell his acid-wash denim jacket was a tad too light for Peachwood Grove's chilly late afternoon.

Passing cyclists in cozy sweaters greeted him, their voices in cheerful harmony. "Mr. Jones!" They chorused in unison. The line of cyclists rode off in the sunset, most waving cheerily. Hellos came from folks across the street, those getting home from a long day's work. Some laughed on doorsteps with grocery bags, while others faintly responded.

Walking alongside Mr. Jones, Joanne took in the urban layout of the town—the precise arrangement of trees in concrete planters, dividing one building from the next. Their design was reminiscent of glossy magazine photos of major cities, places she'd dreamed of but had never been.

There wasn't a doubt in Joanne's mind that she would. Roasted Beans Coffee Spot had started so small but was slowly expanding. With three branches in Sweetgum, she was ready for more, and Peachwood Grove was the next logical step. Big cities would know her name soon enough.

"Hope you're ready to stay out late." Mr. Jones held a clipboard of information. He pulled on his fading blue hat, then scratched his gray scruff of a beard. "Because we have a lot of places to see." He kicked on some yellow leaves while avoiding a fire hydrant.

Joanne kept her eyes forward. A streetlight flickered on the very end of their path. They'd take the corner after getting there. "I don't mind. As long as I finish this tonight," her watch beeped when six p.m. rolled by. She'd be driving an hour to get home, and work was still awaiting her. "How many places are on the list?" She rubbed her hands together, seeking warmth. She'd put this off for too long.

The old man visibly slumped. He peeled through pages while humming. "Six. They're all really good options for small businesses due to location *and* size, but I'll get down to that when we visit each and every one of them." His attitude brightened just now as if he'd remembered his role as a sales agent. "There's another coffee place on the other side of town, so you might have some competition once you open. Not to discourage you, but just a heads up."

She nodded, having done her homework. "I'm aware. But I think there's room for one more." A gust of wind sent leaves dancing and a passerby's hair into a frenzy. Impatiently, Joanne checked her watch again. "We might want to hurry up a bit. Are those sneakers good for a quick jog, Mr. Jones?" She accelerated her pace.

"Hey! Slow down, girlie!" His laughter echoed behind her, even as he tried to keep up.

Joanne paused, brushing hair from her face. "Sorry, I just…"

Mr. Jones got to her at last. "I wish we could've parked closer, but all the spots are taken." He panted, then bent over. "But I'll try to make do with my old man legs, all right? Just don't leave me behind. Remember who knows this town and who's just visiting." He flapped the clipboard like a wing. "Now, let me tell you what I know before we get there."

~

THE OLD THRIFT store didn't quite hit the mark for Joanne. Its limited parking, coupled with thin walls and a low ceiling, was off-putting. Plus, the noisy car repair shop next door? Not ideal. She was used to her branches being cozy spots where customers could relax with a hot drink, and she wasn't willing to compromise that ambiance.

Joanne arrived at the next spot and gave a dusty couch a good smack. Out scurried a bunch of spiders. Jumping back, she accidentally bumped into her escort. "Oops, that wasn't very smart. I didn't expect that," she chuckled, feeling the creaky floorboards give slightly under her weight. "This was a casino once, huh?" she mused, looking out a window obstructed by broken wood slats. Right next door was a roller rink, and directly across was a mall. And upstairs? A bustling arcade, from the sound of it. Footsteps and chatter echoed down the stairwell, with faint music from above. As she walked past Mr. Jones toward the counter, she noticed its once-vivid red now dulled by a layer of dust. The draped sheets over the furniture behind made it feel eerily like a haunted mansion. "Good thing I'm not a kid anymore," she thought, "or this would freak me out."

"Yes. Quite a popular one in the eighties, actually. But of course, it shut down, and no one thought to buy it out." Mr. Jones squeezed his clipboard between open hands. "You look like the type to turn this fixer-upper into quite the venue. With the mall so close, I think this just might be—"

Joanne shook her head of loose curls. "Pass; not feeling this one." She was searching for that just right vibe. Her gut instinct? It was her guiding star, and it was saying, "Keep looking." Trusting it had always worked for her. "What's next on the list?" she asked.

"Yes, ma'am." Mr. Jones crossed the casino off his list. "I think you'll like this next one much better," he said, briskly following her when she glided out.

Joanne rejected the derelict community band room as well as an old trailer outside a general store. Each one had something she liked, but something else she hated. She dismissed the properties, either due to their size, ambiance, or her own intuition. Time flew by, but she would not settle for mediocrity. She knew that her first attempt at branching out in a new town had to be flawless. Joanne had a vision.

As Joanne cruised past, the twilight farmer's market was wrapping up, with a few farmers packing their stalls. A large canopy sheltered rows of fresh thyme, lettuce, and green onions. She watched a woman in an apron head out, a box of pinecones in tow. Checking the dashboard clock, which read eight-thirty p.m., Joanne mused, "Late night for a market."

The convertible, with Mr. Jones at the wheel, meandered down the avenue, its path lit by the muted glow of streetlamps and shadowed by grand oak trees and imposing buildings. They passed Peachwood's beauty salon and barber, continuing until they reached the very end of Market Avenue. Parking was a breeze at this hour.

With a firm *clamp*, Joanne's door shut behind her. The click-clack of her boots kept rhythm as she circled her car. Up ahead, Mr. Jones was already at the door of their next stop, keys in hand. Before her stood a broad, one-story building with an inviting vibe. She took a step back, framing the building between her hands and assessing its potential. "Nice. Right near some hotspots," she noted, referencing the salon before twirling around to spot a bakery and a tech store across the street.

"Come on in, Miss." Mr. Jones slid inside with his clipboard.

Joanne ended her assessment to head in. The square red-bricked design brought her back in time. A younger her would always accompany her mother on errands. Errands that sometimes brought them to the local post office.

"As you can see, we got a real fixer-upper on our hands with this one, but it's a good buy, if you ask me." Mr. Jones just hit the lights. Not a lick of furniture remained. Stray envelopes could be found in corners, but apart from them, there wasn't much left to say this was a post office.

Dust filled the air as she moved to the room's center. Windows lined the walls, some cracked, others missing panes. She scanned the ceiling, noting water stains, bulging spots, and missing tiles. As Mr. Jones continued explaining the place's history, Joanne found herself momentarily distracted by the state of the room.

"… used to be a real sight back in the day, but now it's just vacant." Mr. Jones strolled across the space. "Got walking room," he fanned dust away with his clipboard while going to a window. "Nice view, fresh trees out front, and a lot of spots for furnishing," he singled out six areas where booths could be placed. "It's a little dusty—"

"A little?" Joanne never suffered from allergies or a sensitive respiratory tract, but right now, her eyes watered. She felt burning in her nostrils and needed to clear her throat. "It's like I'm asthmatic," she sneezed in her jacket.

The older man laughed. "So what? You don't want it either?" he asked in clear amusement. "This is the last place on our list. We do have other commercial properties, but these here are our best. At least, for what you're asking," he smiled smartly at her. "Not that I'd ever force you to take something you don't want, but this place was quite the treasure back in the day. Heck, it's pretty nostalgic to Peachwood Grovers. Reminds us of…" he sighed wistfully. "Simpler times."

Joanne didn't mean to seem skeptical. "Oh, I wasn't saying I had a problem with it." Her gut approved of this setting. "It's spacious, charming, well-placed, and an overall good buy." She hit her stomach. "I like it, and my gut does, too." From the time they'd encountered that market, she'd grown attached to Market Avenue. *And the place looks pretty darn good.* She stomped and dust clouds flew up. Specs hid between crevices of each portion of wood. "It'll take some work, but I think this might be right." She sneezed again.

"You sure?" Mr. Jones looked surprised. "You want our old relic?"

Those words had her thinking. "Will people be mad if I renovate this property?" Starting trouble in another town was far from her intentions. She just wanted somewhere nice to sell coffee. So far, this dilapidated post office met all her criteria. "Is it especially dear to Peachwooders?"

"It's 'Peachwood Grovers,'" he clarified with a chuckle. "Many here will likely appreciate a fresh gathering spot. Coffee's your specialty, isn't it? There's nostalgia tied to 'Posty', but that sentiment might be stronger for us who've been around a bit longer. The younger crowd? They'll probably be thrilled with a new coffee joint." He slid the clipboard under his arm, his expression shifting to one of concern. "These youngsters seem to favor coffee over a proper meal nowadays." He exhaled heavily. "But is this the place you're looking for?"

Joanne confidently tilted her head up, hands clasped behind her. "Absolutely, Mr. Jones," she replied, putting on her most persuasive tone. "At Roasted Beans Coffee Spot, we don't just sell coffee. We promote indulging in pastries and delightful treats alongside our beverages." She flashed her most charming smile.

Mr. Jones blinked in amused surprise before bursting into laughter. "All right, you've sold me," he chuckled, guiding her towards the door. "I'll shoot you an email with the agreement and relevant paperwork so you can have a look at them."

"Sure," Joanne had a good feeling rising inside her. *First Peachwood Grove, next, the whole world!* She smiled in satisfaction.

CHAPTER TWO

$\mathscr{I}$t wasn't often that Xavier went into the office. This morning, though, when he'd finished his protein shake and exercises, an email about a certain property caught his eye. So rather than working remotely on other business, he'd suited up for a visit to Sky High Real Estate downtown.

"Let me get that for you, sir." Eddie, the company manager, opened the main office door on his behalf. "We put Jones on the job when she contacted us," he said in response to the inquiry as he hustled alongside Xavier. Ringing phones, modern desk designs, and glass walls bombarded Xavier's senses. This floor stood atop Peachwood's tallest edifice. Four stories below contained a music studio while varying martial arts dojos fit themselves in floors between.

"I know," Xavier gave pleasant greetings while searching for Jones, but felt bothered. He'd never take it out on these hard workers, though. His unsaid preferences pertaining to who bought his properties were unbeknownst to them. So far, he owned three buildings, with two currently being rented out; that post office was his last on the market. *Not anymore.*

Navigating through a maze of cubicles, he finally spotted Jones, who was wrapping up a call. "Jones?"

"Mrs. Gregory, I'll have to get back to you," Jones said cheery goodbyes before hanging up. After fixing the brown tie hanging over his buttoned shirt, Jones stood, causing his seat to roll back. "Xavier! The man himself. How are you, sir?" he asked, reaching out and shaking Xavier's hand.

"I'm quite well. We missed you at game night at the plaza."

"Missed?" Eddie was only a few years behind Xavier. He'd finished college with a degree in management, so had instantly got the job after applying. "I was actually glad to win at something without Jones around," he said as he tapped Jones on the arm. "But our star agent was off working after hours."

"That sure is right," Jones beamed. "And I did it again. The client already signed the agreement. We just need your signature and mine to proceed. Did I mention she's opening a business? Our little town is going to have its own coffee place on Market Avenue." He high-fived Eddie, then folded his arms. "I sent you an email about it this morning. Did you get the time to read it? I see you're all suited up," he whistled while staring Xavier down. "New shoes?"

The young investor cracked a smile. "Yes, they are," Xavier said smoothly. "In your email, you mentioned something about the client I hadn't known until I read it this morning."

"And what might that be?" Jones's thick, graying brows crinkled as he leaned toward Xavier. "Is something the matter? I thought you'd be glad someone was interested."

"It's not a big deal. I just didn't realize that the person you were selling it to was an outsider." He breathed in deeply, letting his pectorals expand as fresh air rushed in. They throbbed from his earlier workout, but the tall man always welcomed the after-effects of good exercise.

Jones looked lost. "Is that a problem?"

"Outsider?" Eddie clicked his jaw, then rubbed his bearded cheeks. "What do you mean?"

"Obviously that she isn't from here," Xavier didn't mean to snap, but he just hated the idea of some out-of-towner profiting off his hometown. Peachwood meant everything to him. These people raised Xavier into who he was and had his back after his dreams were crushed ten years ago. In his darkest hours, the smiling faces of Peachwood Grovers uplifted his drooping spirits. He wasn't sure how much he trusted some stranger among his people.

Jones scratched his arm. "She's not from too far. It's just the town over: Sweetgum Meadows. That nice little place with the festivals and hiking spots. I've visited a couple of times."

"That place?" said Eddie. "Is she moving here?"

"No. I already said why she took an interest. It's a commercial property. She wants to open up a branch of her coffee shop here in Peachwood. Last time I was in Sweetgum, her business didn't exist, but she's young. Probably only opened her little business about two years ago. Seems like a nice girl. A bit picky but ambitious," Jones gave a firm nod. "She has my seal of approval," he raised a sure thumb for emphasis.

Eddie seemed convinced. "There you have it. It's not some corporate vampire coming in to change things. Just a nice girl and a coffee shop," he said as he clasped both hands. "We could use a place like that here, don't you think, Xavier?"

Xavier had already familiarized himself with her intentions. "Yes," he agreed verbally, but thought otherwise. "I think I'll pay Sweetgum a visit first," he thanked Jones and Eddie for their time before leaving. *A girl with a dream and coffee. Who* was she, and did she have Peachwood's best interest at heart? He'd been in the business long enough to know that even humble establishments could grow corrupt. His paranoia might have been irrational, but Xavier couldn't help it. *Joanne Richards.* Who was she?

THE ENTRANCE to Sweetgum Meadows was marked by a sign adorned with painted sweetgum leaves. They swirled and danced around the letters, forming a tapestry that made the words 'Sweetgum Meadows' pop. Xavier was instantly captivated by the artistic touch—a unique blend of nature and craft that transformed a mundane welcome sign into a work of art. He couldn't help but wonder about the hands behind such an exquisite piece.

As he drove further in, the dense canopy of pine trees that flanked the open road began to thin out, giving way to the unmistakable signs of urban development. What was once nature's playground now stood transformed. Instead of towering trees, there were now sprawling malls, buzzing eateries, and other recreational spots. While Xavier appreciated progress, he felt a slight twinge of nostalgia for the untouched beauty he imagined Sweetgum Meadows once was.

Driving along Main Street, Xavier gripped the steering wheel with one hand, while in the other, he held his cell phone, displaying an email from Jones. It detailed everything about Joanne's enterprise — its name, branches, locations, and even her impressive yearly earnings. He mentally whistled in appreciation. The numbers didn't lie; she was evidently quite accomplished. Achieving this level of success, especially before hitting thirty and primarily on her own, was commendable. Clearly, Joanne was a force to be reckoned with in the business world.

But for Xavier, business acumen wasn't the only criterion. Her intentions for the property in Peachwood, a place he and his fellow townspeople considered a treasured relic, were what truly mattered. Yes, he'd acquired that old post office with eventual resale in mind, but it wasn't just any building to be handed off to the highest bidder. Its new purpose needed to resonate with its rich history, and its new owner should be someone who recognized its deep-rooted significance.

The soft chime of his smartwatch interrupted Xavier's thoughts as his feet touched the pavement. A quick glance confirmed the reminder of the eleven a.m. meeting, one he'd already rescheduled. Straightening up, he briskly adjusted and re-buttoned his suit jacket, keenly observing the building before him.

Its vast glass windows reflected the town's charming essence, while the quaint chalkboard by the open door showcased the day's specials in whimsical handwriting. Above the entrance, the shop's name, Roasted Beans Coffee Spot, was elegantly scripted, beckoning patrons inside. The entire setup seemed to call out invitingly, "Come, stay awhile."

And as if the visual appeal wasn't enough, the rich, intoxicating scent of freshly brewed espresso wafted out, wrapping around him like a warm embrace. Xavier couldn't resist; he decided a cup of that aromatic promise was worth indulging in.

"Welcome to Roasted Beans Coffee Spot. How can I help you today, sir?" chirped a young girl at the counter, her hair playfully tied up in pigtails. Xavier quickly scanned the interior, noting that it was relatively quiet with just one other patron—a young man, likely a college student, engrossed in his work by the window.

The café was a harmonious blend of soft, earthy tones: taupe cushioned booths paired with honey-colored wooden floors. Its design and layout, while distinct, radiated warmth and comfort, reminiscent of the upscale coffee spots he'd frequented in more metropolitan areas. A certain renowned brand, a titan in the coffee industry, floated into his thoughts. He mused silently. *She's not mimicking them, but the inspiration is evident.*

"I'll have an espresso," he declared, glancing at the overhead menu before sliding a twenty-dollar bill across the counter. "Keep the change."

"Thank you, sir. It'll be just a moment. May I have your name, please?" The girl's attire caught Xavier's attention. The uniform — a mocha-colored cap paired with a matching apron over a cream T-shirt with honey-hued sleeves — complemented the cafe's warm interior. While familiar, it still held a unique charm that set the establishment apart. He decided not to overthink it.

"Call me Alex," he responded with an alias, choosing a table nearby. The ambient sounds of the coffee shop filled his ears: the rhythmic grinding of fresh beans, the occasional clang of pots and pans from what sounded like an adjacent bakery. Beneath the counter, a clear glass display showcased a delightful array of baked goods. Cookies, cupcakes, croissants — each looking more tempting than the last. Xavier placed his hands on the table, a smile sneaking onto his face despite his attempt to remain impartial.

His drink arrived in a rich brown cup adorned with a contrasting black band and a matching sipping lid. Glancing at the pseudonym he'd given, he took a sip. An involuntary "Mm" escaped his lips. The deep, nutty richness of the espresso enveloped his palate, warming him from the inside out. Xavier typically enjoyed savoring his drinks, taking in each nuanced flavor, but this particular brew was irresistible. In mere moments, the cup was empty. He pondered if there was a proprietary blend that Joanne guarded zealously or if the barista behind the counter was just extraordinarily gifted.

Okay, Joanne, he mused inwardly as the hum of the heater became more pronounced. The cozy ambiance, combined with the lingering warmth from his drink, threatened to lull him into a gentle nap. Shaking off the drowsy sensation, he straightened up, brushing a hand across his face. "Roasted Beans Coffee Spot certainly lives up to its reputation," he remarked, sliding out of his seat.

Discarding his empty cup in a bin near the counter, Xavier nodded in appreciation to the staff. It would have been interesting to meet Joanne in person today, but perhaps it was for the best they hadn't crossed paths yet, especially considering the plan formulating in his mind.

Pushing open the door, he stepped back out into the morning. Two delivery boys were ferrying boxes into the neighboring ice cream parlor. Pulling out his phone, he dialed a familiar number.

"Xavier?" Jones picked up promptly.

"Go ahead with the sale, Jones," Xavier instructed as he settled into his car, inserting and turning the key. The engine purred to life beneath him. "Roasted Beans Coffee Spot will be a fine addition to Peachwood. I just need to oversee the transition."

Jones was silent for a moment, the hum of his office in the background. "Oversee? What do you mean by 'overseeing' the transition, Xavier? Should I let the buyer know you'll be doing that?" he asked cautiously. In all their years of working together, Xavier had always been hands-off once a deal was finalized.

Xavier's fingers drummed on the steering wheel, his eyes focused on the road. "No. Don't tell her a thing and don't worry yourself either. I want to be involved in ensuring Roasted Beans integrates well into Peachwood. Not as a businessman, but as someone who cares about the community," he clarified.

Jones sounded intrigued but also a touch skeptical. "That's rather unusual for you. You've always maintained a certain distance after the paperwork's signed. Why the change now? Have you met the owner?"

"No, I haven't met her, but there's something about Roasted Beans," Xavier began, his tone thoughtful. "I believe it has the potential to be a cornerstone for Peachwood, not just another shop. It felt... different. I want to help bridge the gap between Joanne's vision and what Peachwood holds dear."

Jones hummed thoughtfully. "Interesting. Well, every entrepreneur has their vision, and while your involvement might be well-intended, just ensure it's welcomed. And remember not to overshadow her perspective."

Xavier smiled, his gaze lingering on the rearview mirror, capturing the fleeting sight of Roasted Beans. "Understood. I'll approach this with care and respect. I'll call you with updates."

The conversation left Xavier contemplative, the weight of his decision sinking in as he drove on, his anticipation palpable as he envisioned his plan taking shape.

CHAPTER THREE

Joanne was constantly driving between Sweetgum and Peachwood, and her gas tank was feeling the strain.

Looking over the progress, she remarked, "It's coming along great. Just make sure there aren't any stains or damage when you finish up," her hard hat sitting over her two-strand twists. Only four days had passed since her purchase, and 'Roy's Constructors' were already making significant headway. She had vetted nearly five local carpentry crews before settling on them for their clear expertise. They diligently followed her precise instructions, tearing down unnecessary walls and ripping up the outdated flooring. Joanne wasn't just an observer from the sidelines; she was right there with them. If a mallet swing seemed too wild, she stepped in to correct it, and if someone's efforts lagged, she was quick to get them back on track.

Joanne had mapped out every phase of this journey, breaking it down into seven distinct steps. Seven milestones she intended to hit before opening her doors.

"Understood, ma'am," replied a robust woman perched atop a ladder, addressing the dilapidated ceiling. As she swapped out the old sheetrock for new pieces that Joanne had hand-selected, other members of the crew tackled the kitchen. Joanne had just inspected their work laying the tiles, choosing earthy tones that mirrored the warm ambiance of her Sweetgum coffee shop. When it came to painting, she was determined to envelop the space in those same hues, ensuring continuity between her establishments and creating that welcoming vibe she was known for.

Standing in the lobby, Joanne surveyed the ongoing construction of the wall that would soon separate this area from the kitchen. The door would be added later. She gracefully maneuvered around a few workers laying tiles near the left wall and made her way toward the exit. Her fingers danced across her phone screen, quickly navigating to her preferred online furnishing store app.

With a soft exhale, Joanne skimmed through her top choices for furnishings. "Considering the lighting and color scheme I have in mind, these should be perfect. But those," she mused, "they have such a unique charm." While she aimed to retain the familiar ambiance found in her Sweetgum locations, Joanne was also eager to infuse this new branch with its own distinct flair. She knew that making each of her shops too distinct could be a misstep. However, giving each a unique twist? That was pure gold in her playbook.

Joanne dashed out of the building, the brisk air and wind hitting her face immediately. Overhead, she could hear the rhythmic pounding. She looked up, a surge of pride washing over her as she spotted her signature sign, fresh from her go-to sign company back in Sweetgum. Roy's team was up there, working the ledge, securing the sign with drills and bolts. A few feet away, the crew's electrician quickly worked on the wiring.

Using her fingers to frame the sight, she zeroed in. "Perfect," she exclaimed, satisfaction evident in her voice. The team followed her precise instructions, positioning the sign between the building's wings. Once again, her keen attention to detail had paid off.

Joanne, propped against her car, watched a group of locals strolling by with takeout bags. "Is that going to be a coffee shop?" one of them asked, stopping in his tracks. The small group moved back, eyeing the establishment and unintentionally crowding near Joanne's car.

Ever since the renovation began, curiosity had bubbled among the residents. Her crew had mentioned the numerous questions they received. Joanne smirked to herself. *Can't really blame them*, she mused; this town's about to get a whole lot cozier.

With a swift motion, she produced a handful of business cards. "That's right," she said with a confident grin, addressing the intrigued group. "Roasted Beans Coffee Spot. We open in three weeks. Make sure to spread the word. And hey," she added, leaning slightly forward, "if you know anyone looking for a job, let them know we're hiring. Interviews start soon." The group looked at each other, then back at her, clearly taken aback by her spirited pitch.

As they examined the card, the ambient sounds of traffic filled the air, with cars passing by and engines humming in the background. Two more people walked past while digesting her soon-to-be-hit coffee place. "Roasted Beans Coffee. Opening soon." Joanne handed them a few cards, too. *Lunch hour is perfect for marketing.* People were up and about in search of a meal. She didn't believe in waiting to advertise. Getting the word out as soon as possible was genius.

She gave some more cards to other citizens when her phone dinged. "Tell your friends! Opening soon!" She leaned on her car again as the people gradually dispersed. The sidewalk across the street seemed like a better place to find prospects, but she remained steadfast in her position. In case something went wrong with construction, she needed to be right where she was. "Hello?"

Joanne listened as the plumber she'd contacted about setting up the bathroom told her about his available dates for inspection. "Perfect. So next week? Great. I'll be there. Everything will be in order by then." She hung up but received another call soon after. "Oh, Court. Did you take a look at the drawings I sent you?"

"Yes, I did. I'll send you an email with my digital drawings tonight. Sorry it took so long. I've been busy arranging the wedding."

"I know. Don't sweat it. I'm just glad you found time in the end." Joanne wouldn't know what she'd done if Courtney hadn't finished. She thanked her friend infinitely for assisting, then hung up the call. "Hey, wait, I have a different flooring plan for over there!" she just witnessed a slip up through the window.

Two youngsters kneeling by an assembling wall just dropped a tile package. With whirring drills, pounding, and hammering going on inside, neither they nor their colleagues heard when she shouted. "That's where the back counter goes! I haven't sketched out the flooring for that!" Joanne ran urgently to stop them.

MOST FOLKS TOOK Saturdays as their time to shop and recharge. Just earlier, her friends sent messages describing their weekend plans. Movies, lunch dates, picnics, and walks. Each had someone to share it with. She truly was happy for what they each found, but no relationship could ever bring out the unbridled joy she currently experienced.

With twenty-one days marked off her phone calendar, Joanne took pleasure in admiring her progress. "We are *right* on schedule for painting." She'd picked out some denim overalls for today's project. Splatters of pink, white, and yellow paint already colored its straps and leggings from her last big paint venture some months ago. That being a recreational activity with Courtney and the girls.

The sound of a door slam behind her parked vehicle overpowered her zooming thoughts of calculations. "This might be the earliest job I've ever taken," a woman wearing something similar to Joanne jumped from a white truck behind her. Daybreak had only fallen thirty minutes ago. Coming out early meant more time for work, but the drawback was extra chilly weather and frosty winds ruining morale.

Four other painters hopped from the open truck. It jerked with motion even after they lined up beside the head painter. Their stuff remained in the boot as they gazed in awe at Joanne's work in progress.

A sense of pride warmed Joanne's shivering limbs. She wore a snug sweater beneath her one-piece, but nothing beat fall chills in the morning. As they spoke, pale yellow leaves flew across the empty street while a cold wind blew by. Seeing such a busy road, this calm felt criminal. Joanne gripped her elbows before finding herself by the locked glass doors. Behind them was a sign saying 'closed.' *Soon, it'll read open.* After this paint job, furniture would come in and everything else would fall into place. She already had several interviews lined up for next Monday. "Looks nice, doesn't it?" she proudly got her key and unlocked the front door. "Now to add color inside. Get the paint ready. I know it looks early, but time flies fast. Come on," she went in and breathed. Apart from uncolored walls, the place looked incredible. Her black front counter, the equipment behind it, see-through containment chambers for pastries on top, and not to mention the polished tiled floors. She flicked on the open lights in her crisp black ceiling.

They brightened her shop immensely. Buttons for temperature adjustments were right below the light switch, so Joanne went ahead and pushed them. She relished in warmth when it spread through the room, then ran out again. "All right people. Let's get the floors covered before we start."

Two ladies walked in with exactly what she meant while the remaining two unloaded brushes, tins, and rollers from the back. Joanne went ahead and helped them with at least the heavy tins. She struggled with two white shades in either hand before resting them outside her front door.

"How involved are you getting here, Missy?" the head woman came out, leaving one worker to set up for the job. She wore a white bandana over cornrows that stopped right above her neck. There was a toothpick she chewed between her teeth.

Joanne's hands itched from holding tightly to heavy buckets. Red marks stretched across her palms. "Not too much," she lied before smiling. "Just want to make sure you guys get everything done well and to my liking. Oh, and you remember my designs, right? Your technical painter has some mugs to draw along the walls. If she needs a reminder, I have pictures on my phone. I can—" she dug through her deep pocket.

"We remember your request, so don't hassle yourself," the woman laughed before staring inside. The protective plastic for the floors was almost spread completely. This company worked fast. It was why Joanne chose them over three others in town. In the end, their speed beat rivaling businesses. Lists and charts were made while making her decision. Sometimes, creating them helped with clarity. For someone like her with a jampacked brain, mapping things out aided immensely in decision-making. "How could we forget when you sent that long email? It was…" the lady spent about five seconds coming up with a word. "Pretty detailed and emphatic," she crossed her arms. "So, how old did you say you were?"

Joanne stepped from the doorway when the other girls brought supplies. Their blocky boots crumpled the plastic after entering. "Twenty-four."

The woman gawked and tapped her own cheek. "Wow. And you've started your own business? Good for you, girl. You're one of a kind. But I have to warn you. Having your own money-maker takes a lot of work and dedication. You seem driven, so I won't lecture you but prepare to work your butt off all by yourself, okay?" she elbowed Joanne in a motherly gesture. "Promise me you won't give up—"

Joanne would take insult to this woman's assumptions if she wasn't grateful for an opportunity to boast. She kept humble on most occasions, but at times like these? Oh boy, did she love naming her achievements. *It's simply appropriate. She needs to be informed.* "How could I when I already own three branches of this same coffee shop in the next town over?" she batted her lashes with sass.

"Thanks for the advice, ma'am, but I'm really not as new to this as you think. I started out *quite* young and kept going from there," she grinned widely with her signature winner's smile.

With wide eyes, the lady laughed before apologizing. "Well, you must have started pretty darn young then," she gave an impressed nod with pursed lips and crinkled brows, saying 'mmm.' "I *love* to see it." With that, she went inside. "Now, let's get your place looking good, shall we?"

"Yes, ma'am," Joanne stepped in behind her, her own boot crumpling plastic when she did.

CHAPTER FOUR

Xavier killed his car engine on Market Avenue that cloudy Monday morning. He'd have to cross the road after getting out since his destination lay on the opposite side of his parking spot. He'd had eyes on it for weeks. During its renovations, paint job, and furnishing, he'd acted as its secret overseer. But its owner didn't even know he existed. At least, not yet.

He got out and waited on the sidewalk. People with umbrellas walked back and forth around him. Some on phones, others bustling, most unaware of his presence. He tried dressing down to not draw attention. He wanted to be seen but not by any locals. Today, her opinion mattered above everything. It was the only way he'd get in there. Inside her world, where he could assist. She seemed completely capable of running a business, but Peachwood wasn't Sweetgum. He knew the place and its people so possessed insight on how to win them over.

A slow-moving bus rolled from up-street as he crossed. The man checked his time while strolling along the other sidewalk, then paused. "Roasted Beans Coffee Spot. Savor the perfection," the circular sign in black and white contained a cup of coffee with both phrases arched around it. 'Roasted Beans Coffee Spot' took the top while 'Savor the Perfection' curved the bottom. He liked it and had actually been present when she first put it up. Joanne behaved just like he'd predicted. Everything from which place her sign went had to be perfect. While parked four cars down from the building, Xavier had overheard her calling dimensions. *Something about three feet from ground level and some inches for something else.* While her carpenters hung the sign, she didn't hesitate to remind where exactly it should go. He loved how particular she was about something so minor, but wondered just how receptive she'd be to outside suggestions with that attitude.

He pushed open the door to enter, and a mind-numbing warmth enveloped his body. *Looks just like the others.* He spent some time digesting the décor, then found something distinct. *I stand corrected.* He went to the wall-lining the booths, then smiled. Small paintings of coffee mugs and steam were near every table. Come to think of it, new coffee stickers lined the windows, too. Xavier backed up and admired them. This wasn't like her Sweetgum branch at all. *Just a couple of additions doesn't mean it's all that different.* Everything else matched perfectly. From the color scheme to its heavenly aroma. *Only that there's no one upfront right now.* The sign read 'CLOSED,' but a 'HELP WANTED' sign hung over it.

Xavier dinged the silver bell up front before waiting. *I would have done a few things differently.* He liked her business card promotion strategy, but while she did get a few heads turning, with them came skepticism. Confirmation that the new coffee place wasn't locally owned bred doubts across town. Xavier had overheard quite a few discussions at meetings. Questions as to who Joanne was and whether she was stealing opportunities from residents took off like jets in the atmosphere. Civilians were hesitant to trust Joanne and her business, just like he'd predicted. Peachwood Grovers were... territorial by nature, but for good reason.

In the past, some bigshot company nearly opened a factory in town but ultimately failed when Xavier bought it out. Not a soul had agreed to having toxic fumes pollute their sweet home. To this day, his fellow Grovers still commended him for using his wealth to protect them. Now, that old factory was a school. The second one in town. One could argue that Peachwood residents were traumatized from that last invasion, but Joanne obviously had better intentions than greedy businessmen. *Because she's not that. She's a greedy businesswoman!* He chuckled at his own joke. *She's not greedy.*

If placed in Joanne's position as an outside business, Xavier would have gotten acquainted with other small business owners for their seal of approval. Sally's Salon and Michael's Eatery were nearby. Joanne would have better luck here if well-known local businesses could vouch for her. Peachwood trusted Peachwood and Peachwood alone. Sure, Mr. Jones spoke well of her whenever she came up, but that was one word against hundreds of skeptics. Xavier told a few friends he'd liked her coffee, but not even that swayed them. One or two curious cats might visit for a cup, but a few customers weren't enough for good business.

The back door creaked open. "Sorry for the wait," a woman in an apron and jeans met him up front. With hands spread across the counter, she snapped her fingers. "You're here for the interview," she said, as if enlightened.

Xavier for once had no words. Until now, he'd only seen her from afar.

Joanne's round-shaped brown eyes blinked confusedly. Her even complexion and rich dark skin tone radiated the bright colored lights on this dingy gray morning. She wore a black cap with her business name in white letters. From it came braided pigtails stretching just a little beyond her shoulders. Small hoop earrings hung from her ears. Gold hoops that matched a thin necklace hanging over her black rounded collar. "Sir? Did you come for the interview?" she asked slower.

Xavier caught himself at last. "Yes. Good morning. My name is Xavier Evans. It's an honor to stand before you in this wonderful establishment."

"Okay then," she seemed impressed. While she shook his hand, he noted the tenderness of hers. It felt… small in his grasp. Small yet sure, firm. He slipped his away when they finished shaking. No nail polish painted her shortly cut nails. "Follow me to the back."

~

COMFY, he rested himself in one out of two soft-cushioned chairs in her office. They'd gone through the bakery before coming here. Another door nearby led to what he presumed was the manager's office. His future office if he played his cards right this afternoon.

Joanne clasped her hands behind her name template. "So, Mr. Evans, I took a look at your application form. Your cover letter, especially, seemed quite convincing. You sound ready to die for Roasted Beans if it means getting its name out there." She rolled her chair forward. A few unpacked boxes lay around the room. Behind her was a window displaying the view outside. Just an empty alley and chain-link fence. Nothing particularly breathtaking.

He thought about the words written on his cover letter. He promised booming sales with skills he'd learned through prior managerial roles. He'd managed a skate park after college, but just for three years. His career as an investor kicked off quite soon following that. Even in college, Xavier had begun saving toward his now successful business. "That's because I am," he said smoothly. "I've already started plans on how to do just that," he plucked a folded page from his pocket. "Here. I think you'll find my ideas worth considering."

Joanne arched an eyebrow before stopping him. "Hold up," she reclined while holding the arms of her chair. "You haven't gotten the job yet, sir. I appreciate your enthusiasm, but we can talk plans *after* you receive a position at my business. Am I clear?"

He should have expected this response. "Crystal," he placed his suggestions back where he'd taken them. "I suppose that's enough proof of how eager I am for this position. I've heard talk around town about your place," he tapped his thumbs. "People like the design, but I've heard a few doubtful remarks here and there. I guess I just really don't want such an amazing café to be overlooked. Plus, it helps that I'm a big fan of coffee," he said, hoping he wasn't laying it on too thick.

To that, she frowned, sitting upright. "Well, it *won't* be overlooked, so you have nothing to worry about." She placed her hands on her desk. "Your application also mentioned past management experience at a local skate park. A job you had for three years, I believe?" she brought it up like an issue. "Can you tell me what you've been doing between then and now?"

Xavier preferred hiding his true profession as long as possible. "I believe I did clarify that I've worked remotely since then," not completely wrong. He did oversee some companies for friends out of state. Never for long, of course. They mainly contacted him to oversee and manage fresh businesses. He'd depart from affairs once the company found its footing. "I mentioned a few overseas establishments."

"Yes, but you've only managed them for short time periods. One for six months, this real estate company in Dubai for five—*Dubai?*" Joanne blinked several times. She zoomed in on her phone screen.

"Ha ha ha," Xavier shifted in place. "And now you can surely understand why I don't stick around long at these establishments. They've paid me well. The owners only got in touch for my close inspection, anyway. Sort of to hear my advice as they navigated difficult times." He watched how her face morphed from surprised to suspicious.

Joanne put the phone down. "So, you think I need your advice," her expression said she wasn't pleased.

He maintained his cool. "Look, the people I've worked for in the past were just friends of mine who thought my knowledge would be useful in achieving their business goals. I'm by no means an expert who thinks he can take over, but I think that if we work together, Roasted Beans Coffee Spot can have quite the positive impact on

Peachwood." He crossed his legs confidently, smiling though she scowled.

It took a while, but Joanne's face softened. By no means was she grinning, but she seemed less pressed. "Well, all right then," she took a deep breath. "If I were to hire you, what are a few things you'd do to ensure the smooth run of my café?" she seemed to dismiss their prior topic.

Xavier prayed she really had. He didn't need her suspecting his true intentions here. *I've given away too much.* What if she dug into his resume and found out that the companies he'd managed belonged to investors? It wouldn't take much to trace back to him. He wasn't sure how she'd react to the truth, but so far, she struck him as someone who detested lying. Technically, he hadn't told a lie yet, but withholding details could count as such. "I'd first of all deliver free coffee and pastries to business owners nearby. To gain their support. I think getting employees to stand outside with samples might help as well and, oh, perhaps setting up vending stands at local events might be a great idea to draw people in. I've lived in Peachwood my whole life. I know a thing or two about its people. They like community and warmth. If we extend a hand, they'll take it, and before you know it, business will boom." He took note of her blandness throughout his explanation. *Joanne Richards sure is tough.* He might have started things on the wrong foot, too.

Joanne's brows creased in what Xavier read as consideration. She snapped her fingers. "I like the free samples idea, but everything else sounds desperate."

Wow. Xavier blew a puff of air from his mouth. "Trust me," he said with conviction. "If we take that approach, results will come before you know it. Peachwood is a tough town for aliens. Especially—"

"Aliens?" Joanne interjected. "Why that term? And you didn't answer my question. I asked how you'd ensure the smooth run of my café. Not how to get business." She drummed her fingers on her desk.

Xavier didn't flinch. "I was getting to that. And about the 'alien' comment. It's well known you're not from town, Ms. Richards. I didn't mean it offensively."

Joanne waved a hand in dismissal. "Okay, fine. Now tell me your plan," she sat back with crossed arms.

"Gladly." He was more than happy to share.

CHAPTER FIVE

With the opening three weeks away, Joanne's main focus was preparing her staff for the big day. She'd already settled issues with supply orders, stocks, and purchases, so she could now show her handpicked employees how to operate their tools. They'd not only need to handle coffee makers but also cash registers and yogurt machines. Stressing the importance of team work took first place on her list. All of these were essential for work to run well.

"And remember, don't mix that up with the croissants, although they look similar. If you look closely, they have a different tone from one another," she spoke behind the counter after lunch a week later. She intended for training to last seven days. They'd already knocked four days out of seven off their calendar. Her teenage workers carried a special zeal. These kids were fresh out of high school and looking to make ends meet at college. They asked many relevant questions during sessions, which Joanne appreciated.

"Okay, and what about the two tarts? Because the strawberry and cherry tarts are the same color," someone pointed out with their hand raised. Joanne had put out samples from their menu. They covered the counter in boxes.

Joanne nodded. "There'll be blue food coloring on the bottom of the cherry tarts," she used tongs to lift one. "See?" the staff droned a collective 'oh,' then took notes. Only one boy seemed unprepared in that regard. He'd always ask someone for paper when the note-taking started. He also spent most of their sessions leaning by the coffee makers. Staying in the back seemed to be his preference. *Whatever,* Joanne would judge him based on his performance, not his behavior, throughout training. She'd dealt with enough employees to know that nonchalant workers sometimes worked best. They absorbed information like sponges and put their colleagues at ease in high-stress conditions. *But not everyone's the same.* "Okay, so we went over everything on the menu. You guys know how to make both espresso and classic coffee, so... let's take questions then call it a day for training. I know some of you have classes," one hand shot up from the back. "Oh." Her good attitude plummeted the second she saw him. *I was starting to wonder why he'd been quiet all day.*

With great effort, Joanne buried her distaste under politeness. "Yes, Xavier?" from the second they'd sat down together, she'd known he'd be difficult. She would have chosen the other interviewee if it weren't for Xavier's undeniable passion. She wished more candidates had come forward as potential managers, but that wasn't the case. Back in Sweetgum, she'd have loads of applications flooding her emails when a new branch opened. Pedestrians would call out to her, too, asking for a spot. But here in Peachwood? *Nope. We're not doing that.* As much as it pained her to admit, Xavier's words had left an impact on her: what he'd said about Peachwood and its people. She hadn't felt alienated until that word rolled off his tongue.

Xavier wore a white sweater over his broad upper body. It sucked on his muscles, creating a detailed picture of his solid pecs. He wore dark jeans over black leather shoes. She'd seen him every day this week and, quite frankly, was sick of his natural good looks. He had a well-trimmed beard on that face of his. That chiseled face that always wore a smile. Slender brows, slanted brown eyes, long lashes, broad nose. At this rate, Joanne could draw him. He always seemed to find himself in her personal space, staring down either pleasantly or inquisitively. His rich, dark complexion complimented his eye color and full brown lips.

"We went over the whole cup system yesterday, including how to refill the paper cups for coffee," Xavier guided her to the cups stacked behind them. They stayed by the coffee makers, on a black desk at the back. "And while I do like how they're arranged with each one inside another, I think that organizing them this way could pose an issue on busy days if employees are particularly scrambling," he picked a cup off another. "Easy for me to do since I'm not stressed, but look." He grabbed several, and others tumbled down.

Joanne bit her inner lip as people agreed with him. "Well, that can happen with anything if you're not careful. Mistakes are normal. That doesn't mean there's an issue with our cup organization." Was this guy for real? Did he not hear himself? It had been this way for every session. If it wasn't the register, it was the coffeemaker, and if that wasn't a problem, he hated their uniforms. She couldn't tell if he had it out for her or genuinely wanted to help.

Xavier shook his head. "I think it does mean there's an issue. My suggestion would be to line them up so it's easy to just pick one and fill it before fastening the lid," he demonstrated by spreading out ten cups with ease before taking one and holding it under the coffee dispenser. "See that? So, one of you will be tasked with that, too. Who wants to do cup lining?" He stood beside Joanne while searching for hands. "You want to do it, Charline?"

"Okay, no," Joanne gently brought Xavier back to his place, then dusted her hands. She heard giggling from their young staff but ignored it. "The cups will stay how they are because they've been that way at all my other branches and have worked fine," she emphasized the word fine to Xavier. "*I* am in charge, so trust me on this. It doesn't mean I won't hear your suggestion, but in terms of minor details such as cups, I don't think we need to argue," she clapped. "Okay, so—"

"I actually think that these so-called 'minor details' *do* require our attention. That's how you gain success in every aspect of business," Xavier stopped her to say. He faced the trainees while holding the counter. Once again, he'd put himself on Joanne's level; up front and central. "Imagine if one of those chairs had a short leg," he waved his arm over the lobby. "Don't you think it would say something to our customers about what we stand for?" He connected his fingertips while everyone whispered.

Everyone but Joanne who was *this* close to snapping. Luckily, she had more self-control than that. "Yes, but that's not the same. Of course I'd fix a rocky chair in the main room. It's an *actual* problem."

Xavier crossed his arms. "What about if the chairs were too close? Or we kept them from the window even after realizing that our customers love looking outside?" he shrugged. "Technically, there'd be no obvious issue with seating arrangements, but it could be improved. We *could* move their seats towards the glass or leave it alone because—" he flicked his wrist lackadaisically. "Ah, it's not an *actual* issue, so why bother?"

With every word said, Joanne's patience slipped. Meanwhile, Xavier's authoritative approach somehow seemed mischievous. At least to her. He wasn't smiling or laughing, but that face and that twinkle in his eyes. His face displayed neither anger nor malice. She could only read their absence as mischief.

She tapped her palms before squeezing them. "As you can see, Mr. Evans, we have quite a collection of seats lining the windows, so you have nothing to worry about regarding that."

Xavier put arms at his sides. "I'm *not* worried about that. It was just an example."

"Okay, but that example is not at all similar to your cup arrangement non-issue, so I'd prefer if you'd refrain from stealing time from our other employees who likely have questions of their own but haven't had the chance to ask because of your…" Joanne held back from insulting him. "Your enthusiasm is greatly appreciated, but like I said, this is how I've done it at my other branches, and it works. Remember," she tapped the buttons on her blouse with a soft palm. "I'm in charge."

This time, Xavier hesitated. He walked back to his place among the staring employees with a tiny smile. Concrete evidence of what Joanne suspected. He *did* take pleasure in undermining her authority. Or maybe she'd embarrassed him. No. Someone like him didn't seem capable of feeling such a thing. Then why the smile? "I know," he said shortly. With an open hand, he bowed his head, saying to proceed.

Joanne hated how he felt the need to grant permission. If he played around too much, she just might seek outside assistance. There had to be someone willing to move here from Sweetgum. Lots of people would die for this job. She may have gotten carried away with that expression, but Sweetgum folks liked her business. Her reaction to Xavier's meddling might have been strong just now, too. He wanted to help. That she appreciated. "Okay, good. Now, does anyone *else* have questions?"

A hand that wasn't Xavier's went up.

Relief washed over Joanne when she saw it. "Yes?"

A girl, slightly leaning on the counter, read from her notes. "I just wanted you to go over the coffee-making process if that's okay, because I'd like to get it right."

Joanne had no problem doing so. "Of course," in seconds, they assembled in the back, which wasn't far. Xavier's new cup arrangement hadn't been packed, so Joanne simply took one for instruction. She asked one boy for the bean bag before briefing them on whipping up quick, delicious coffee in record time. More questions came up in the process. She gladly responded, then packed up Xavier's mess. "Okay, but at the end of training, we're going to try that for real, okay? With real ingredients so you guys see what it's like that way."

To her great disappointment, among the nodding heads came a pointing finger. "Ms. Richards, if I may just…" Xavier popped up beside her like earlier. He traveled so quickly she hadn't seen him move.

No! No, you may not! Stop interrupting me! "What is it, Mr. Evans?" Joanne had gotten an A in high school drama. She knew a few things about acting. Especially in the presence of someone who irked her. Except Nevaeh. When Nevaeh got on her nerves, Joanne let it rip. But exploding on friends and exploding on colleagues was different.

Xavier touched the two coffee makers. "Don't you think we might avoid mishaps if these weren't so close to the bakery?" He stretched back in search of something. "What if this table went over there instead of here? Or somewhere near the back hall, perhaps?" He grabbed the table and dragged it.

Screech!

Everyone covered their ears at the deafening racket. Joanne stopped Xavier from moving any further. They had some feet until he arrived where he wanted, but she hauled the table back to its place. "What are you doing? No discussion or meeting? Just act? You can't… why would you do that?" This took first place as Xavier's most irritating action.

Xavier stood tall. "My apologies, Ms. Richards. I just wanted you to see how much space we'd have if we moved it over. I just think that with our pastry makers leaving the bakery and register handlers moving back and forth to relay information, that having the baristas so close might breed mishaps," he used arm gestures to highlight his concerns.

Something broke in her brain, but Joanne didn't show it. "Again," she inhaled. "This is the exact arrangement of my other successful branches," she said slowly. Joanne found herself in Xavier's face. She couldn't reach with how tall he was, but with a raised chin, she saw his eyes. "And judging by the word 'successful,' I think that it works. No one slips up, there're no problems, and business runs effectively," she said softly. "Your suggestions are appreciated, Mr. Evans, but please remember which of us owns this shop and which of us has never worked at a coffee place in their life."

The man scratched his short, tapered beard. "I'm not so sure if my suggestions are all *that* appreciated, seeing how dismissive you are of them." His lips stretched at the corners while the staff members giggled.

Joanne had no time for his games. She stepped away with a gentle smile. "I'm sorry if it seems that way, but for everything you've said over the course of training, I've actually taken notes." Those words weren't completely true, but they weren't false either. "Anyway, please remember that I'm in charge here, Mr. Evans. I'm in charge, and I know what I'm doing." She refused to break eye contact.

It took about five seconds before Xavier nodded. "I know."

She watched him find a spot among her other workers. *I know.* If she had a dime for the number of times he'd said that... "All right. No more questions? Good. Everyone can head off. Great training, guys. Can't wait for opening."

CHAPTER SIX

As a token of welcome, Joanne had given Xavier a desk calendar when he first arrived.

He wrote an 'x' over yesterday's date and counted three boxes to another. This one being decorated with pink markings and stickers. *Opening.* Joanne wrote that herself. He spun his seat around.

The back window displayed a gray fall morning. Training had ended last week. Apart from Joanne's frequent scolding toward him specifically, it went exceptionally. Xavier didn't mind Joanne's chastisement. In the end, she'd taken at least one of his ideas into consideration. *Only what I said about changing the 'OPEN' sign, but it's a start.* He saw them doing great things together once she opened her mind to more suggestions.

An orange leaf stuck itself in a muntin of his window. Xavier twisted his lips at the sight before rising. He walked the carpeted floor until he reached the back wall. There, he slid the window open and got the leaf by putting out an arm. "There we go," he twirled its stem while cold air came in. The heat from his office clashed against it, forming atmospheric tension.

Knock, knock, knock, she always knocked thrice. "Come in." Xavier closed his window. He walked around the desk and leaned against it, fixing his tie and running a hand over his fresh haircut. His chest buzzed when the door opened, but he hid how he felt.

"Hey," Joanne's perfume wafted off her puffed-sleeve blouse. It reached her wrists. She wore black dress pants and heels to complete her look. He'd gotten used to seeing her in uniform. This get-up surprised him when he first came to work. She did say they'd stick to dress codes only after opening, but he'd taken her for more of a 'dress down' sort of lady. "So, I've been thinking," she carried a folder and pen.

"You've been thinking..." Xavier repeated. She looked annoyed that he'd done that. "Sorry, ma'am. Proceed." No one else unleashed his jocular side like she did. He admired Joanne but found her too stiff. This was by no means a flaw, but sometimes rigidity was intimidating.

Joanne looked him over. "Why are you standing in front of your desk?" She quickly surveyed the room. "Your stuff looks settled in, but you're standing. Is the chair uncomfortable? I ordered great quality." Her heels squished the carpet as she walked around his desk. "It's the same as mine. Plush, leather."

"There's nothing wrong with the chair, Ms. Richards," he said to relax her. "I chose to stand because you came. I didn't mean to alarm you." She twisted his seat by the headrest, examining the material. "Ms. Richards?"

Joanne stopped. "Okay. If you say so." She opened her folder and put it down. "Do you remember your idea about bringing coffee to local businesses?" she picked up a flier bearing their logo. A date, time, and location were in the corner as well.

"When did you make that?" He took it, loving the design. A cartoon coffee mug floated before a black background while every letter came in red. "Roasted Round-Up. Oh, we're visiting local businesses?" he smiled. "Is this an announcement?"

"Mhmm," she sounded smug. "I've been working on those for a while, actually. I'll get Charline to deliver them this afternoon, but first, you're going to prepare a list of some local businesses for me.

You'll also help me put our drinks and snacks together on the day of the event, okay? I'd ask some employees, but I think the manager should be the one who helps me out." Joanne stood behind his chair. She linked her hands on top of it. "So, are you available this Friday or what?"

She didn't need to ask. "Of course. If it's for you—I mean work. By that I mean work. If it's for work I'll be there," he winked suavely to which she didn't react. That made him chuckle. "So, you admit that my ideas aren't completely bad, right? You called that one desperate."

"Well, after some thinking, I realized it was genius," Joanne smiled shortly. It disappeared when she walked to the door. "I'll be hosting the event while you'll be there to serve and support me however I ask you to," She turned to face him as she reached behind her to open the door. "I told you I appreciated your suggestions and that each of them stuck with me, didn't I?" She raised her brows, then left. "It will certainly be an event for the books!" she called from the hallway.

Xavier found himself in the doorway. He watched her strut to her office in fascination. *It sure will be. I'll make sure of it.*

Cookies, *tarts, cupcakes, bagels...* Xavier ticked items off a clipboard. Sunlight hardly shone into the room. He didn't mind coming in so early for preparations, but being out of his house before six a.m. felt surreal. He'd completed his workouts at four rather than five. *All for Joanne.* Or work, rather.

"Come hold the vacuum cup for me while I pour this coffee," Joanne called at his back. She, too, was behind the front counter. He'd inhaled the aromatic scent of fresh coffee while packing pastries for today's activity. A translucent blue box would hold their samples. Joanne had requested he carry it while she held their cups and flask in an insulated lunch bag they hadn't yet packed.

Xavier clicked the plastic box shut and left it on the counter. "No problem, Ms. Richards," he found himself by the back table in no time. There, he quietly observed as she poured carefully. At first, his attention was glued to the wide, red steel flask in his grasp, but eventually, his eyes wandered, resting on her face.

Joanne fit the kettle back after finishing. "Screw the cap back on," she wore a suit this morning. An all-black pantsuit with pointy high heels. Her hair was different. She'd gone natural for the occasion. The low bun worked wonders for her face. He liked how clearly he saw it with her hair off of her forehead. She was absolutely gor— "Why are you staring like that? Bring it to the lunch bag. I told the call center we'd be there at eight. It's almost seven-thirty, and we haven't packed up the espresso."

He blinked at her interruption of his admiration. "Oh, right. You're so right." He rushed to the counter. After resting the flask inside the chosen lunch bag, he went back to help her with pouring. "This smells so good," he'd sneak in a compliment right now. "Did you come up with the recipe yourself?"

Joanne put down the kettle and shoveled coffee beans into the maker. "No, I found it online—of course I came up with it. Why would I open my own chain of coffee shops if I didn't have something special to offer?" she raised another vacuum flask among those she'd lined up on the table. There were four in all. Two for coffee and two for espresso. She'd already told him which color was for what. *Red flasks for coffee and blue flasks for espresso.*

He unscrewed a blue flask when she told him to. As she poured espresso into it, he thought of how this arrangement came about. "I just know they'll enjoy what we bring." During the week, they'd worked together on getting word out about their visits. He'd sent emails and answered queries. "Did you finish your opening?"

Joanne smirked. "Of course I did. I practiced about fifty times, too. I think they'll be engaged." Her eyes twinkled when they connected with his. "This isn't the first time I've gotten creative with advertising. Icebreakers are like second nature to me. I was pretty good at them in high school, too."

"Is that so?" He liked that she shared this. His heart skipped a beat. "So, you're one of those star presenters?"

"Oh yeah," she finished with the flask and snapped her fingers. "Come on." She walked across to the other desk and coffee maker. There were four in all. "Carry those with you. We're making good time, but I have warm-ups to complete before we present."

Xavier picked up the flasks and sped-walked behind her. "Warm-ups?"

"Vocal warm-ups so I don't choke," she paused by the table. "You should do some, too. Your voice is a little husky this morning. Not that it's noticeable, but *I* notice, and it's irking me, so at least drink something before we head off." The young woman wrapped her fingers around the kettle handle before slipping it out. She filled a flask with coffee when he held it.

Xavier eyed the gold bracelet she wore. It slid past her suit cuffs just now, adorning her wrist. Why was he noticing these small details? *I guess I'm just captivated by my boss.*

"Did you hear me, Evans?"

He returned to reality. "Sorry, ma'am. What was that?" *click* went the flask when he closed it. While opening another, Joanne repeated herself.

"Your role is to hold up each menu item while I call them out and nothing else. So while I present, you'll stay in the back and do that, okay?" she spoke slowly and with an overly pleasant flare. He'd annoyed her enough to know that she behaved this way when irritated. He would admit that her self-control amazed him. *Too bad I can tell she's aggravated.* Another person might be fooled.

Xavier smiled at her lovely grin. She had this vein that poked out of her forehead when irritated. Was she aware of it? "I'll be on my best behavior, Ms. Richards. You have nothing to worry about." He wouldn't make any promises, though. Everyone they'd be seeing was a friend of his. He knew what they liked, and cold presentations weren't it. "Can you give me a bit of a preview of your icebreaker? It's the only thing we haven't practiced," he said.

With a click and a clunk, Joanne put the kettle back. "And that's because it's not a 'we' thing and more of a 'me' thing." She raised her brows. "Anyway, we're almost done, so let's not lose momentum." She helped him with packing the flasks then gathered some cups. After concealing them, she pulled her insulated bag over her shoulder. "Just know that when I start listing, items on the menu," she patted his chest.

Xavier felt a rush of warmth through his body when her steely eyes made contact.

"You just hold them up," she smiled. "Got that?"

"Yes, ma'am."

"Excellent." Joanne lifted a portion of the counter. "Now let's go. Good job. You did well today," she whistled while walking past tables.

Xavier picked up the pastry box and went after her. "Thank you. We make a good team." He watched her stride confidently to the door.

Joanne held it open. "We do, don't we?"

He hadn't anticipated her agreement.

"When you do as I say," she added, a tight smile making an appearance on Joanne's stony face. "Anyway. We're behind the clock. Out, out, out," she ordered.

Xavier left with a shake of his head at her bossiness. "Of course."

JUST LIKE THEY'D PLANNED, Xavier acted as Joanne's assistant for their presentations. She led while he stayed behind the lunchroom counters, watching her lose favor in every place they visited. Xavier understood Peachwood Grovers and had predicted their reactions. Joanne behaved too formally for their liking. Peachwood was a warm town known for its friendliness. No one here wanted some stranger listing menu items to them. They preferred being involved and getting to know their addresser.

Joanne allowed comments after each visit, but that couldn't make up for her lesson-like format. They'd so far visited a call center, beauty salon, and supermarket. Currently, he stood silently as she aimed her pointer at the packaged cookies he held behind yet another cafeteria table. This one being at the local pet store near Peachwood Park. The drive here took a bit longer than their other destinations.

"You get this adorable chocolate chip delight free if you purchase two coffees in one day. On its own, it's just fifty cents and quite the treat. Our special cookie recipe ensures that each one of those chocolate chips will melt in your mouth." The room had an echo despite its small size. There weren't many tables to move, but those available were currently pressed against the left wall. Employees shifted benches to sit in front of them. Some stood around while others peeped through the door.

From Xavier's vantage point, they seemed disengaged. Someone just checked their phone, and another person hid a yawn. From management to store clerks had gathered for this. They'd closed temporarily just to lend an ear to Joanne, but she wasn't capturing their intrigue as much as she should. At least to Xavier. So far, their audiences seemed most attentive when the samples went around. Now and then, questions popped up, but Joanne made sure to remind them that questions were only allowed *after* her speech. He understood her reasoning, but it sometimes put off their listeners to be shut down that way.

The store manager scratched her head up front. Xavier knew her from school. He watched how discreetly she glanced at her watch and decided to do something. "Hey, didn't you guys hear her?" He walked around the table and met Joanne in front of it.

Joanne seemed surprised but didn't drop her smile. "What do you mean by that, Mr. Evans? I'm sure they hear me just fine." A million questions raced behind her widened eyes. He saw her annoyance but mouthed 'trust me' before continuing.

Xavier shook the plastic bag pinched between his fingers. "*This* cookie right here comes free on opening week, so long as you buy two coffees in one day! Isn't that incredible? Not to mention, those chips just *melt* in your mouth. Mm," he ripped it open and took a big bite. *Wow,* it really *did* taste amazing. He rolled his eyes to the back of his head in exaggeration, summoning giggles. "No, it's actually that good. Try some, Pete," he plucked another off the table and tossed it at the assistant manager. "Guys, I'm seriously not over-selling here. Roasted Beans Coffee is out of this world, but our cookies are too."

Joanne grew quiet as Pete chewed the treat. Previously distracted employees now turned forward in wait of Pete's reaction.

Pete licked melted chocolate from his lips, then sucked some from his finger. "Mm. That's a good cookie right there," he said to their manager. "Try it."

Xavier grinned triumphantly, watching as others asked for a bite. "Hang on now. That's just *one* of our pastries. The others are amazing too, but you'll definitely want to buy more coffee on opening week after your first cup because just the smell of Roasted Beans Coffee is to *die* for! You smell it, right, Lisa? What about you, Claudine? Tate?" He addressed people while the cookie went around. They started complimenting the immaculate scent and requesting samples. "Everyone will get their share, but let me introduce you guys to a little treat I like to call 'jelly tart.'" He kissed his fingers.

While Xavier proceeded to show off their menu, Joanne made some attempts to take over. He let her get a few words in now and again, but ultimately dominated their presentation. At their next stop, it was the same, even after she told him to revert back to 'background support.' Xavier would have listened if he hadn't seen a stark difference in reception. During sample distribution at both the puppy store and Downtown Deli, they'd gotten more questions pertaining to opening. People came to Xavier specifically for details. That could have been because he was friends with everyone they presented to or his amicable presentation style. Either way, more folks were showing open interest. In Xavier's eyes, this was a win.

A gentle sunlight radiated from above at lunchtime when they finished.

Xavier shut the trunk with a merry whistle. "Done just in time for lunch, huh?" he said to Joanne. They were in the parking lot of a local megastore. He'd once again stepped up as the main presenter earlier. About ten staff workers confirmed they'd 'swing by' on opening day after he'd promised more free samples if they did. Some promised they'd visit just to say hi. Quite a bit of Mega Store's workers played football on Saturdays. They made up Peachwood's local team known as 'The Grove Giants.' He liked those guys and appreciated their support.

Joanne walked to the driver's seat after pressing her car key. She silently sat down, slamming her door.

He startled at the aggression. As two cars rolled into empty parking spots around them, Xavier found his place beside her. After dragging on his seatbelt, he watched her in silence.

She started the engine before sitting back, facing him in clear annoyance.

Xavier put on a smile, though upset by her attitude. "I don't understand. Didn't you hear how exhilarated they were to visit?" he asked as she turned on the heat, which hit him like a pillow of comfort. He nestled into his seat. "Ms. Richards, this is great for business. I think we might have a full house now that we've personally asked for people's support. We did great today. The people are interested. We'll have enough buyers for the week. I'm certain," he hid a soft laugh at her clear disaffection. "They know our business. That was the whole point of coming out today, wasn't it?"

Joanne twisted herself so they were face to face. Her seatbelt stretched on her shoulder. "*My* business!" she shouted.

He'd seen her angry before, but nothing compared to now. Had he gone overboard? "Okay, yes. Your business, but we did this to get *your* business name out there, and it worked. Ms. Richards, I see no reason for dissatisfaction." He watched her windshield wipers swipe leaves from the glass.

Joanne pulled the combination switch to stop them, then unbuckled her seatbelt. She had freedom to face him without restriction. "Yes, we got the name out there, but we could have done that *without* you overriding my presentation. Without you specifically ignoring my requests to stay quiet and without you having long-winded conversations with *every* single person we met at our stops." She held up her phone. "We were supposed to stop at noon. It's almost two p.m., Xavier! You ruined my schedule! I had other engagements that I've had to push back because of your… disobedience. How many times do I have to say that I am in charge here?" she folded both arms with a head cocked sideways.

Her anger infatuated him in inexpressible ways. Those fiery eyes, her scrunched nose, and intense glare. He did find her argument ridiculous considering how successful their meetings had gone, but his attraction was undeniable. *I'm not attracted to her; I just admire her passion.* He'd die on that hill of denial. "Ms. Richards… I'm sorry, but I've said it before, and I'll say it again," he perched an elbow on his seat's backrest. "In Peachwood, we're swayed by genuine appeals and friendliness. Your presentation style was just too cold. I could see we were losing potential buyers with your method, so I stepped up," he readjusted his sitting position. "Wouldn't you say that our last three audiences showed more interest than our firsts? It's because of my—"

Joanne waved a hand in dismissal. "No, no, don't give me any of that," she gave a stern frown. "The only reason they 'seemed' more invested when you took over was because you insisted on pausing every so often to make conversation. Xavier, you distracted them from the products. They were engaged in *your* small talk. Not in my coffee or pastries. So don't you dare try to act like you did right in there." She stared through the windshield with folded arms, shaking her head in what Xavier perceived as disbelief. "I don't understand. Do you think I'm incompetent at my job? Is it that you think you're smarter? Are you a chauvinist at heart?"

His chest ached at the very strong term. "What? No. No, Ms. Richards, don't say that. I promise you I'm not." He hated where she took this. "I do respect you. I have *so* much respect for you it's almost distracting, but—"

She looked into his eyes with her deep brown irises. Without thinking, Xavier gazed into her eyes, getting lost in her questioning stare. She enticed him beyond reason. Although it pained him to know he'd caused these uncomfortable emotions, he found them gorgeous while exhibited by Joanne. Xavier would much rather see her smiling, though. "Listen, my respect for you is the reason I sometimes do too much, okay?" he said with clasped hands. "I truly want this business to succeed. In my mind, *every* single thing that I do is for its betterment. Sometimes, I come up with ideas on a whim because I think they'll help your success. I enact them because that success is all I care about. So, I'm so sorry if I've offended you, but it's really not because I think less of you. Not at all. *Absolutely* not. I just care deeply about Roasted Beans Coffee Spot and satisfying its owner." He hoped this heartfelt explanation might ease her irritation.

Joanne said 'humph,' before buckling up again. She put her hands on the wheel and then pressed the gas pedal. "I'm no fool, Mr. Evans," she drove forward at a quick pace, jerking Xavier into the back of his seat. Thank goodness for seatbelts.

As she drove past parked vehicles to enter the bustling street, Xavier observed her profile. "I know that you're not. No fool would have started a successful chain of coffee shops before the age of thirty. You don't need to tell me you're not a fool, Ms. Richards. I know."

"You might just be saying all the right words, so I'll lay off you."

Xavier had a good laugh. "I promise you I'm not," he breathed easier, seeing that she no longer frowned. "I meant everything I said. Would I really go out of my way like I have the past few weeks if I *didn't* want your success?"

She seemed unmoved. "I don't know. You seem to believe that I don't know how to acquire said success and need your help even though *I'm* the boss. You can't be so tone deaf that you don't realize how poor this looks on your part, Mr. Evans." They drove faster when traffic cleared, but stopped at a red light. A pack of pedestrians crossed the street from a nearby cinema. They seemed to be a teacher taking her class on a field trip. "I'll agree that we scored loads of prospects today, but we could have done that with my method too. *Just* saying."

Xavier breathed, smiling. "You did have a clear speaking voice when you took charge, but like I said, Peachwood—"

"Yeah, yeah, friendliest town in the world and you know your people better than anyone because you lived here your whole life. I get it but what do I keep saying as your boss who's methods have proven successful?" Joanne leaned sideways with an ear out, driving smoothly through clear roads.

Xavier brushed his forehead, amazed by her stubbornness. "You're in charge, and to trust you. Got it."

"Good," she smirked somewhat evilly. It appeared so to Xavier, anyway. "Now start acting like it."

What a woman, was all Xavier thought as she cranked up the heat.

CHAPTER SEVEN

"Clara Wilson? Your coffee's ready!"

"Can I get that without milk?"

"Add one of those chocolate chip cookies in the bag for me."

Customers, customers, customers. Their 'Closed' sign had been flipped to 'Open' at sunrise. Just thirty minutes past six, they saw their first customer. From there, the rest came flooding in. It was safe to say that 'Roasted Beans Coffee Spot' attracted a crowd this cold opening morning. Their employees worked tirelessly behind and at the counter, making buyer satisfaction their priority.

Joanne helped out to ease the pressure. She wore the shop's uniform while filling cups with coffee. "Get that to the customer waiting by the door. She looks impatient," she ordered a staff worker. When the girl did so, Joanne sighed with relief. Relief was short-lived since an order for decaf coffee came from up front.

"Make that two decafs!" the cashier hollered while handing out change. "For Robert Louis," he told the man to wait in a booth while a second customer came forward. His line moved pretty fast. On top of having two coffee makers in the back, they also had two registers up front. A register on the far left and the other on the right. Currently, one was manned by the boy who'd just spoken while their manager—Xavier—operated the other.

"Of course." Joanne snuck a glance at Xavier while preparing the drink. She had a partner assisting. Together, they worked at breakneck speed.

"He said Robert was his name?" a server left the front to pick up that last order. She shouted after appearing since conversations buzzed in dozens. All sorts of people gathered in large numbers for coffee. Some wore business suits, others dressed casually, while oddballs wore extravagant getups. Likely attendees of Peachwood High. Teens adored fashion.

Joanne heard confirmation from her assistant on the server's question. With eyes on Xavier, she fit the lid on Robert's second coffee. "Here." She handed the server the cup, then marched over to Xavier's station. "Hold it together for a second, will you, Fiona?" she said to her assistant.

"Ms. Richards, I don't know if—" Fiona's pitch quivered while Joanne walked with purpose.

"Espresso for Paula!" another order came in after Joanne left. She by no means intended to leave her worker stranded for long. There was just something she needed better sight of. "Cletus, go help Fiona," she stalked past three boys assigned to handle orders on Xavier's end. *Wait,* Joanne walked backwards. "Why aren't you boys preparing coffee? We have a full house and it's opening morning."

At first, they babbled varying excuses before settling on one explanation "We're just waiting for the next order," Cletus fixed his black cap over thick twisted braids. He jogged across like Joanne wanted and joined Fiona.

Joanne could not fathom what that meant. "But the line is packed!" She flung an arm at Xavier, who looked deep in discussion. The man at the front of the line listened as Xavier expressed himself.

"Packed and not moving. Xavier takes a while before taking

orders," another explained while holding an empty coffee flask. He rested an arm on the machine while his partner tapped his thumbs on his phone screen. Their laid-back attitudes contrasted greatly with Joanne's side of business. What was this? A free-for-all?

You have got to be kidding me. Joanne ground her teeth in response to this information. "Fine, but look sharp in case an order comes your way. And don't use your phone on the job. Only in case of emergencies," she stepped towards Xavier with arms crossed tightly. Just like her, Xavier also wore the company uniform. Its red sleeves covered his defined arms and complimented his frame.

Xavier called an order for an iced coffee before saying 'next.' When a pleasant old lady appeared before him, he bared his teeth gleefully. "Mrs. Monroe. So good to see you up and about this morning," he struck up conversation immediately.

Joanne watched from behind as Xavier talked and talked to the sweet old lady. Meanwhile, more buyers entered their main door. Two fit themselves in Xavier's everlasting line, while three joined the shorter one. *Of course, they would.* Why was Xavier being so slow? Was it deliberate? She couldn't deny the old woman's smile while Xavier addressed her, but that didn't change how bad for business this could be.

She rapidly tapped his shoulder. "Mr. Evans," Joanne hissed.

He only now detected her presence. "Hey, boss lady," Joanne had never seen a happier man. "Business sure is booming, isn't it?" Beside him were two girls handling pastries. They lifted them with tongs to place them in small paper bags.

"Yes, it is," *no thanks to your slowness.* Why did she believe he'd change after their heart-to-heart three days ago? He hadn't overrun anything since, but surely, this behavior counted as disrespect. At least a form of it. Then again, Xavier didn't seem to realize his own fault. "But you need to—"

Someone in an apron and hairnet came to Joanne. "Ms. Richards, there's an issue with the stove. It won't heat up past two hundred degrees," she folded her gloved hands with a shaken expression. "I promise no one tampered with it. For some reason it just stopped working."

Joanne could not *believe* her ears! "The stove stopped operating?"

Xavier called for a second order before his next customer showed up. "I wouldn't panic if I were you, Ms. Richards. They've made enough to last until lunchtime," he winked, seeming uncaring in Joanne's eyes.

"What do you mean to not panic? This is a disaster!" Breathing felt impossible all of a sudden. "Okay, no. I won't lose my mind." Joanne tapped her cheeks twice. "Call this number, okay?" she got her phone then went to the bakery. Xavier would have to wait. *He's right, though;* they did make enough to last all morning. At least on a typical morning. Today was not typical, but she supposed they'd be okay. She always advised pastry chefs to prepare for 'the worst.' Not to the point that they'd waste ingredients on slow days, but just enough for a busy one.

Joanne entered the bakery with squinted eyes as hot air hit like gusty winds. She'd take a look before their maintenance man arrived.

HER KEYS JINGLED while locking her office door. Joanne's handbag was on her shoulder as she fastened the lock and stepped back. "What a day," she caught Xavier doing the same, now grabbing his office door handle. He wore a backpack which crumpled the sleeves of his uniform. She would admit he made it work. Even though Xavier himself had voiced disapproval of its design.

"I know." Xavier's lock clicked before he tossed his keys upward. "Mind giving me the time?" He caught it with ease and stuffed it in the pocket of his crisp jeans.

Joanne hadn't forgotten his attitude earlier. After what she called the 'morning rush,' they'd only seen four customers. Two after lunch and two before closing. Back at Sweetgum, customers came in all day. Since today was only their first, Joanne wouldn't let this bother her. Tomorrow would surely be better now that word spread about her service. Said service could have been faster if someone didn't insist on chatting up their patrons, but she'd discuss that soon. "Eight p.m.," she walked down the carpeted hall to the bakery.

"Wow. Late day, too," Xavier stayed on her heels while they passed stoves and counters. The cleaner had already fulfilled her duty. Not a grain of flour sullied the room. Joanne knew she picked right when hiring. She never missed when it came to employees. Except in Xavier's case. While not terrible, Xavier *did* pose several problems to Joanne. He just… clashed with all her ideals.

After leaving the bakery, they reached the front counter. Both made their way to the exit from there. She'd already locked the back door.

When they left the premises, a chill hit Joanne. She shivered and ignored honking vehicles zooming behind her. Sweetgum differed from Peachwood in that regard. After seven p.m., the streets were clear back home. But Peachwood seemed busier. Although, it might have been the Friday night vibes keeping Peachwooders active at this hour. "Xavier, listen," she pocketed her keys.

Blaring headlights shone on Xavier while a car rolled from down the street. "I'm listening." Just their vehicles remained along the sidewalk. His car seemed fancier than she remembered, but Joanne would not make it her focus.

She adjusted her handbag. "You need to be faster when taking orders." She slid some hair strands behind her ear. The fall breeze just blew them back out of place. Today, her hair went past her shoulders in loose brown coils. "Your line was the slowest this morning, and it really posed an issue. We talked about giving quick service remember? People come in before work. If you stay and chat with them, then they're going to be late. They just want to pick up and leave." She didn't think she'd have to explain this, but Xavier was special.

His brows went up in what she perceived as stun. As for why this surprised him? Joanne didn't know. "They just want to pick up and leave?" He tilted his head. "Are you sure about that?" The man leaned his tall frame against the closed door. "I think that right now, building a connection with customers is essential. If they didn't want to talk to me then they wouldn't," he shrugged, standing straight again. "But they do. Because they like genuine service that comes with a smile," he smiled for emphasis.

Joanne waved her hands around with a shaking head. "No, Xavier. All of that will come later. Right now, we need to show that we're fast, efficient, and tasty. Who wants to stand in line for ten minutes before being served? That's annoying. Especially on busy mornings." She rubbed her arms, now thinking of her long drive back. Out of all the hurdles she'd faced opening here in Peachwood, commuting was the worst. She wasn't sure how economical it was to drive to and from here every day. Just one drive took an hour, and gas wasn't cheap. Also, traveling so far after dark felt unwise. Especially while exhausted. *Boy* was Joanne exhausted.

Xavier scratched his beard. "Have you spoken to anyone who was in line to see me?" To her great irritation, he smiled with cheek. The streetlights illuminated his stretching lips.

"No, but would you want to wait ten minutes when you're late for work and all you want is some good coffee to get you alert?" she walked to her car, sneakers scraping gravel.

Xavier went to his car as well. "Yes. If it meant I'd get a good conversation out of it," his vehicle made a sound when he pressed the keys. "Trust me, Joanne, if the customers hated my style, they wouldn't keep coming to me." He opened the driver's door and sat. "Have a safe drive home."

For a while, she glared, but decided not to argue. Her tiredness would not allow her. If he pulled a stunt like that tomorrow, she'd bring it up again. But for now, Joanne would just leave Xavier alone.

While driving down the freeway, she thought of her predicament. Her radio played old country tunes she'd heard growing up. Joanne put on this station to ease her growing headache. With thoughts swirling in clusters around her frazzled brain, she made a decision. *I'll have to rent a place while getting this location off the ground.* In terms of Xavier, Joanne would deal with him once she solved her commuting problem.

CHAPTER EIGHT

Working under Joanne brought back old memories. Before Xavier hit it big in the real estate world, he'd taken entry jobs like anyone else. While his role here wasn't technically entry-level, his participation in small tasks took him back. In high school, he'd worked part-time as a cashier to 'Shake 'tha Thing,' a smoothie shop at the mall. Meeting customers and serving them with a smile would alight something beautiful inside him. Right now was no different. Even with Joanne breathing down his neck!

Two weeks had gone in a flash. Soon, October would end, ushering in November. He usually involved himself in community activities but hardly had energy these days due to work. Whenever he'd get home from a long day, sleep was Xavier's main desire. To shut his eyes and snuggle with a pillow. He'd been right to put his remote duties on hold. Managing foreign companies after getting home at nine would wither him. He'd missed his golfing club two weeks in a row because of his job. They understood his reason, but the guilt was a monster. At least dodging meetings came with an upside. With his close involvement, Roasted Beans Coffee Spot was doing quite fine.

"Here you go, Mr. Antoine. Thanks for being our number one customer since opening."

Mr. Antoine gladly accepted his latte. Daylight was dimming, giving them just two hours until closing. "Thank you, Xavier. Your coffees give me life. Ha!" He hobbled to the seat he always took when visiting. Right by the door in a single-person booth.

Xavier threw a towel over his shoulder, watching how contently the old man sipped. Other than Mr. Antoine, there were no other customers. They'd had a good morning, but afternoons and evenings had been slow.

Charline wiped the counter while Xavier stared, thinking as the diligent girl hummed merrily. With business being slow around now, employees occupied themselves either with mundane tasks or useless cellphone applications. Baristas engaged in conversation behind him while the pastry servers typed messages on their phones. He couldn't see the bakers out here, but Xavier could guess they'd taken their own personal breaks too.

"Charline," he patted the girl's arm. "You've noticed that Mr. Antoine comes here every day, right?" he whispered. The older man sat at a distance, but Xavier couldn't risk him overhearing this.

Charline slowed her cleaning. "Of course. He says our coffee is the best he's had in years," she said as she tugged her cap bill smartly. "And he's right about that for sure. Ms. Richards' recipe is everything."

"It sure is, but I think we should do something special for him," Xavier saw it now. "He needs to understand how appreciative we are of his loyalty," with a turn of his head, Xavier caught the baristas spying. "Get over here, guys. I have an idea."

Soon, all front desk workers encircled Xavier. He hoped Mr. Antoine would not catch on. Then again, once that old man sat with his drink, the world could burn down, and he wouldn't bat an eye. "You all know Mr. Antoine, right?"

"He has a shoe shop," Cletus pointed out. He wore twists beneath his black cap. "And, of course he always orders lattes here."

Xavier beamed at the mention of lattes. Employees knowing their customers warmed his heart. They'd only just opened, but the staff was alert. *"Exactly.* I'm thinking that in honor of his loyalty, we should rename our lattes to the 'Mr. Antoine Special'," he heard collective remarks of accordance. "I know, right? You guys see that it'd be a great way to show him our appreciation, right?"

"Yes. And other customers will want their own specials too. This will definitely encourage more people to order." Charline bounced her stout body. Her fellow workers reacted similarly, but with varying degrees of exuberance.

"You're very right about that, Charline. *Very* right," Xavier sent her outside to the specials' board. "The sooner we rename, the sooner word will get out. Everyone knows Mr. Antoine, so heads will turn once people see his name on our specials' list," he felt pleased when Charline left the counter. "Everyone else can head back to work, okay?"

Charline stopped mid-way, facing Xavier. "Wait, Mr. Evans. Shouldn't we tell Ms. Richards about this?" She held the edge of a table while tilting her head. To this moment, Mr. Antoine hadn't looked up from his drink.

Xavier spread his hands over the counter. Joanne had told him to watch things while she took a call in her office. Since then, two hours had gone by, and in that time, Xavier had shifted the cups to his preferred arrangement, moved around some pastries, and was now renaming a menu item. He knew she'd at first be angry after realizing these changes, but was sure she'd warm up to them. After seeing that his adjustments improved service, Joanne would surely open up to more. "No. It's okay. She put me in charge while she's dealing with some personal matters, so don't worry about her." He'd overheard her speaking to landlords. Having Joanne be a resident of his beloved town sounded spectacular. Xavier wouldn't mind giving a tour. Maybe then she'd realize Peachwood and Sweetgum's differences.

Charline looked to give his instruction some thought before complying.

"Are you sure she won't be mad, sir?" asked a concerned barista. She sat beside the coffeemaker on a chair she'd pulled from the break room. "You changed the cups, too. What if she gets mad and... terminates you?" The young girl looked terrified on Xavier's behalf.

Xavier quickly waved an arm in an unconcerned manner. "Don't worry about me or Ms. Richards, okay? We'll be just fine." He spotted another customer coming through the doors. "Everyone to work. Come on." This person knew him. With a smile that rivaled pure sunshine, Xavier slid to the register and struck up a conversation.

"I'D LIKE the Antoine special, please." A cheery young woman was their last morning customer. The morning rush ended within an hour due to improved efficiency from Xavier's recent changes. Not just the cupping arrangements were adjusted, but also napkin and paper bag locations. He'd spread them over the pastry containment display for better access.

Xavier could not contain his delight at his success. He watched from the bakery's door as Charline handed Mr. Antoine's drink to another pleased customer. That little menu tweak really got people talking. Almost everyone they'd served started their order with a question about it. Xavier didn't man the register this morning, but supervised who did. Joanne still appeared engaged with other issues, so hadn't come out to assist. What a shame that she hadn't witnessed all he'd improved. He just knew she'd simmer down after seeing their effectiveness. In the end, they both wanted Roasted Beans Coffee Spot's success. Joanne might finally realize his good intentions once facing his positive changes head-on.

"All right, guys! Great morning rush. You all did great," Xavier commended everyone with a round of applause. They clapped for themselves as he went into the bakery, now congratulating their hardworking pastry chefs. Though stunned by its sweltering heat, Xavier remained inside. He insisted on clapping his hands for every employee.

They'd been leaning on counters with frosting-covered aprons, but Xavier's compliments made them stand tall. A few bowed, but most smiled with soft giggles. "In here could be a sauna," he remarked, getting laughs. While moving along the white-tiled floor near narrow steel counters, Xavier heard footsteps outside. They came through the back, leading to his and Joanne's offices.

He ceased motion when Joanne appeared in view, standing in the doorway. Silence fell like a brick. He locked eyes with Joanne, his lost but hers oozing dissatisfaction. Dissatisfaction in Xavier. Or possibly in something he did. *Definitely something I did,* and he knew exactly what.

"Mr. Evans. Follow me to my office," her loose curls whipped when she turned around. He watched them bounce behind her. Even in that tacky uniform, she managed to intimidate him. Or to at least *seem* intimidating. Xavier wouldn't say she was scary. Although he did feel a sense of dread while exiting the bakery. He had his defenses ready, though. Joanne could not deny that business never looked better. He just wished he'd captured the intrigue of each curious customer, all pleasantly surprised by the enhanced menu.

In Joanne's office, Xavier sat down before her large desk. An unnerving chill crawled down his spine as she took a seat, too. He noticed scattered documents covering her desk; her open laptop left in the mayhem. "Is everything all right, Ms. Richards?"

Joanne's seat swayed her body slightly. She steadied herself to roll it forward. "No. Everything is not all right," she used a soft yet stern tone. "Tell me why you renamed our lattes to 'The Mr. Antoine Special' without my consent yesterday? And if you don't mind, could you please explain why—even after I said not to—you went ahead and changed the arrangement of our cups? Not only that, but our napkins and other utensils?" she placed clasped hands before her, brows crinkled in clear annoyance.

Xavier's stomach sank. Seeing her so obviously angered spurred contradicting reactions from him. On one hand, she *did* evoke emotions of fright, while on the other, his soul felt exhilarated. An excitement he'd gotten all too familiar with from working alongside her. If only she knew how crazy she drove him. "Mr. Antoine has been our most consistent customer since opening." He matched her somber attitude. "I just thought it would be nice to show him our appreciation." A gust of wind put pressure on her windows, sending stray leaves against the glass. "He came in today and was pleasantly surprised. Our other customers loved it too. We handed out eight Antoine specials this morning. They loved—"

"And what happens when word gets around and someone in Sweetgum tries ordering the 'Antoine' special? Or someone from Peachwood visits our Sweetgum branch and tries placing that order?" she asked harshly, tilting her head. "Look, you can't just *rename* drinks on the menu. I can't believe I have to say this to someone, but you can't. And as for all the other things you've changed? I'm disappointed. We went over why they need to stay how they are, and yet here you are going directly against what we agreed on," her voice went up in the end. "Xavier," she chopped the desk with one hand. "*Respect* me. *Listen* to me. Stop doing whatever you please when *I* am in charge. Do you know how out of place you're being?"

He gulped. "Ms. Richards, haven't you heard anything I've said?" He smiled shakily. "The special got people talking—and about the cups and napkins? It worked well. It's not like I'm jeopardizing our efficiency. No," he waved a hand in denial. "I'm *improving* it. Today, we worked so much better because of what I changed," her shaking head told him everything. "Ms. Richards."

Joanne held out a hand to him. "Listen, if you keep refusing to manage *my* coffee shop to my satisfaction, I *will* get rid of you. You're not indispensable, Mr. Evans. You're really not. And while I appreciate your passion, you must see why your behavior is unacceptable," she hit her chest. "I have *my* way of doing things. I want my Peachwood branch to follow the blueprint which worked at my other branches, okay? And if you really can't see that working out for you, then the door is *right* there," she extended a hand towards it. "Do I make myself clear?"

Never in Xavier's life had any employer threatened his job. He must have pushed Joanne off the edge. *She definitely isn't playing around with me.* He stared deeply into her dark brown eyes. So fierce she was. Strict and steadfast in her beliefs. His pulse went wild like an erratic vehicle driven by a drunkard. "Crystal," keeping a straight face proved difficult while in her presence. While Xavier had utmost respect for Joanne, he also found her stunning. And quite frankly, he secretly enjoyed riling her up. For a while he'd denied it, but right now, sitting in her rageful presence confirmed everything he'd ignored for several weeks. Xavier was definitely attracted to his boss. Extremely so. "I'll go change the sign right now."

"Good," she crashed her fingers on her laptop keys. "Close the door on your way out."

When standing outside Joanne's office, Xavier touched his chest. It vibrated. *Joanne Richards,* he smiled to himself. If he wasn't careful, she truly would fire him. Though Joanne couldn't see it, he knew his input's worth. An opinionated Peachwood resident's guidance would do her business good. So, whether she liked it or not, he'd continue assisting. *But more subtly.* First off, he needed to get back in her good graces; if he had ever been there in the first place.

"I think I know what to do." He moved slowly to the bakery, rubbing his beard. Joanne wanted a place here, right? He bet if he helped her, she'd feel less angered. He'd sensed her stress levels rising a while ago. It kind of hurt knowing he worsened her condition. He didn't want her miserable. Not at all.

That settled it. His next project was to find her a rental to settle here in Peachwood. She deserved a break, and he owed her.

CHAPTER NINE

Wednesdays were her only days away from Peachwood.

"I have *never* met a more insufferable person. Like, oh my goodness! How can someone be that annoying? I say one thing, he does the other, I try something myself; he takes over. It's like a never-ending cycle of absolute agony with that man. I'm usually way better at hiring, but somehow, I messed up when picking him. Now I have to be there practically every day to make sure he doesn't screw things up," Joanne went on and on that lunch hour at a booth with her friends. To make up for staying in Peachwood so often, she paid a visit to her branch on Main Street today. Her friends agreed to meet this afternoon to say goodbye. This catch-up session might be their last for a while. Her plans to relocate while setting up her new café were already in motion. As if by a miracle, Joanne had found a rental just last night.

Courtney sat beside her holding a mug. Earlier, there'd been a heart in her latte, but sipping ruined the art. "Come on Jo. I bet he's not that bad." As usual, Joanne had a full house at this hour. She and her friends had scrambled for their seats after coming in. They nearly got stolen by jumpy high schoolers who now sat by a window. Garrulous patrons in neighboring seats *and* lines competed in volume with their small group. Something about Roasted Beans attracted droves.

"She's just being dramatic like she always is about work," Nevaeh reclined across the table. She bit her croissant, chewed, then swallowed. "What's the worst thing you've said that he's done? Change the name of a drink?"

Joanne's eye twitched at her passive reaction. "Yes, but people can't just change the names of menu items. I'm not being crazy here, am I?" She sat straighter, her jeans squeaking against the leather chair. "Brandi, back me up here. I have every right to be annoyed with Xavier, don't I?"

Brandi was next to Nevaeh. "I understand why you're mad, Joanne," she said, stirring her iced coffee in its plastic cup. "It does seem like he's disrespecting you from what you've described, but—"

"*Thank* you," Joanne pursed her lips at Courtney, then Nevaeh, who stuck out her tongue. "I'm his boss, but he somehow doesn't care at all what I think. I've spoken to him about his behavior time and time again, yet he just can't take the hint."

"Okay, yes, he's irritating, but I just don't know if it's worth losing your sanity," Courtney said gently. "Joanne, every time we talk to you these days, you've sounded undeniably tense. Even now, you're tense." She massaged Joanne's right shoulder. "Guys, you need to feel her muscles. I've never sensed such tension in my life," she said with wide eyes. "If I were you, I'd handle him by giving him the boot."

Nevaeh clapped. "Yes. You're the boss, so just get rid of him. Even if I do think you're being a little big-headed about it." She dusted crumbs off her hands. "No need to hurt yourself over someone you said is replaceable. But it sounds like you've met your match to me." She pinched off a piece of her snack. "Brands, what do you think?"

Joanne rejected these suggestions before Brandi spoke. "It'd take too long to replace him and things are already chaotic over there," she traced around her cup's rim. "I could start searching for a new manager right now, but I don't know. I do like his passion and work ethic, but man, is he stubborn. How can someone be so…"

"Wait, hold on," Courtney interrupted. "Did you say he was cute?"

Joanne had no idea how this question arose. She heard giggling from Brandi and Nevaeh, but it only worsened her mood. "No. I did *not* say he was cute. What are you talking about, Courtney? This man is driving me insane, and that's all you care about?"

"No, I care about your well-being too, but I just want to know so I can picture someone when you rant." Courtney's obvious coverup wasn't working. It did make Brandi and Nevaeh snicker, but Joanne was not amused. "So, is he?"

Joanne's *other* eye twitched. "It doesn't matter because whether he's cute or not doesn't change the fact that Xavier Evans has given me my first gray hair!" she snapped, drawing attention from seated customers. She groaned with elbows on the table while they slowly looked elsewhere. "Sorry for yelling."

Courtney put an arm around Joanne. "You sent us pictures. They weren't gray. They looked more like a lighter shade of brown." She rocked side to side while wrapping an arm around Joanne to comfort her. "So don't stress yourself about it," she said, letting go to drink a mouthful of coffee.

"Right. Listen to Courtney," said Brandi. A bell rang up front when someone's order was ready. She glanced as they went up to get it, then shifted her drink aside. Brandi stretched her arms across the table. "And if you did grow a few grays, it's nothing to lose your mind over. It happens," she informed knowingly, forever providing wisdom within their group.

Nevaeh wiped her fingers with a napkin. "You should focus on the positive, Jo. Like how that guest house with the nice gate opened up right when you were about to give up on finding somewhere to stay," she said as she crumpled her napkin. "And on how you didn't deny that this Xavier guy is cute," she teased by kissing the air in Joanne's direction.

"For the love of—" Joanne's elbows hit the table. She shielded her face while her friends laughed. "I *did* deny that he was cute because there's nothing cute about being a pain to your boss." she dropped her arms and crossed them. Just one sip remained in her cup, but Joanne felt slightly sick of coffee. At least today, she was.

Courtney twirled a single braid of her passion twists with one finger. With eyes deliberately wandering, she whistled a well-known love song. "I'm still not hearing a vehement 'no' on his looks," she caressed her fresh hairdo.

"See, Joanne? That's another upside. His face is nice to look at. Maybe if he actually agrees to behave himself, you and he can get to know each other," Brandi beamed like sunlight at noon. With her ice cubes clattering in her plastic cup, she sang along to Courtney's little love song.

Joanne's mouth progressively widened. Nevaeh ended up singing, too—out of tune. They were all off-key from each other, further exacerbating her annoyance. "Girls, if you're going to make fun of me through song, at least do it right. Come on. You *know* that song's usually sung in F major. What are you all doing?" Her statement spurred bouts of laughter from each of them. She smiled, loving their contagious joy.

Nevaeh swiped tears from her eyes. "Jack of all trades, Joanne. Topped every class back in high school, including music. I'd give it all up to be as well-rounded as you. Seriously," she said as she flicked a hand in front of her face, rolling her eyes. With her snack finished, Nevaeh picked up her chilled coffee.

"Ambitious *and* successful," Brandi corrected.

"Thank you guys for the compliments, but this man's looks are not an upside, in my opinion." Joanne flattened some loose strands of her curled hair. It went past her shoulders in dark brown loops. She gently tossed some to her back. "But I will say that the guest house is definitely an upside. I didn't expect such a nice place to open up right when I needed it. I like its affordability."

Courtney held tight to her mug handle. "The universe is giving you a break. It's probably a sign that things will look up soon. Don't lose hope, okay?" Her other friends contributed to Courtney's optimistic interpretation. Their positive words alleviated some inner strain aching Joanne's muscles. "And maybe Xavier isn't actively *trying* to annoy you like you think. You mentioned that he said he wants to help, so he probably really does. The things he's done have seemed pretty interesting from a business standpoint," Courtney added.

"Hmm," Joanne rubbed her own shoulder. "I don't know," Nevaeh and Brandi upturned their lips as if considering Courtney's words. She'd entertain the prospect longer but grew tired of this discussion. "Anyway, Court and Nev, how are the wedding preps coming along?" She'd do the honors and change the subject. Visiting Sweetgum was her chance to forget. All drama and stress back at Peachwood could stay there for now. Ranting helped immensely with easing stress, but lamenting too much posed risks. She'd hate to head back more weary than she'd left. So, right now, Xavier could remain an afterthought. Something to handle another time. Though she cared deeply about her new branch, there was more to life than obsessing over its success.

"... so we'd get to see him then!" Nevaeh shouted.

Joanne didn't catch anything before that. "Wait, what?" she asked, taking in her friends' smiling faces. Mischief twinkled in each of their eyes. "I thought we were talking about the weddings."

"We were, but you know Court and Nev are taking their time," Brandi continued playing with her icy remnants, shaking her cup. "So that was how we ended up talking about the highschool football game next week. I just realized it's Sweetgum versus Peachwood."

Leaning forward, Nevaeh started rattling words Joanne at first missed. "Hey, wait, slow down," Joanne said to her ecstatic friend.

"Guys, you know my brain is all over the place. There's a football game?"

Nevaeh groaned. "Yes. Keep up, Jo. Come on." Though her anger irked Joanne, she didn't comment. "And it's going to be our chance to meet this Xavier guy."

"Are you kidding me?" Joanne cut through their cheering. "Why are all of you so hung up on him?" Her words meant nothing. They continued rejoicing over this fact. How were they so sure Xavier would even be there? Joanne herself usually enjoyed sports, but with so much on her plate, she might just stay home. *Knowing Xavier, he'd definitely go.* That guy knew absolutely everyone in Peachwood. But without Joanne's presence, her friends may have difficulty pinpointing him. *Oh well. I need to put me first.* So, for once, she'd sit out a fun sports match.

CHAPTER TEN

Xavier commended himself for convincing Joanne not to sit this game out.

"Foul! Foul!" the referee dropped his whistle with wild gestures, leaving his post as two players untangled themselves from each other. Blinding lights, angry fans, and harsh comments from both sides shot across the field. It seemed like the real deal tonight, this match. In terms of energy, Xavier felt legitimate. Like a true sports fan watching a professional showdown, even though it was only a high school game. Everyone was serious about this game between the two rival towns.

"Enjoy your coffee, Mrs. Foster," he said, handing one of the parents a cup. Although he was enjoying the excitement, he'd come here to work. Xavier had constructed this stand earlier in preparation for a busy night of vending. At first, Joanne absolutely refused his idea of serving at the game, but with much coaxing, he wore her down. It still surprised him that he'd actually convinced her. She'd been so hellbent on staying home.

"Thank you, Xavier, you're such a sweetheart," Mrs. Foster left the line with a hot cup. In this cold temperature, folks appreciated affordable drinks to keep them warm. Even with the game in full swing, their stand drew many. Customers from both Sweetgum and Peachwood left their seats to purchase coffee. Spectators bundled in large coats, gratefully accepting drinks when given. As they chatted, their breaths appeared as white mist.

For him, the cold wasn't a bother since serving hot drinks kept him toasty. He and Joanne's matching jackets helped as well. They bared the Roasted Beans' logo on the left breast. Its material wasn't so thick, but handling hot cups and kettles made up for that.

"Hey, hey, don't get distracted," Joanne muttered, carrying two cups to his makeshift counter. "I don't want you chitchatting when we have so many in line." As usual, she used a clipped tone with him. Her brown curls left her cap through the back in a ponytail. "Here." She brought more cups and set them down. With just the two of them working, the expectation was slow service, but Joanne didn't allow that. When they'd run out of pre-prepped coffees, she'd made more in a flash. For a second, he'd silently marveled as she worked like lightning. He loved Joanne's drive, but other aspects of her business approach rubbed him the wrong way.

Like this, he watched her slide to his left and hand out two coffees to a well-known carpenter. Her stony expression vanished, replaced by the most 'customer service' smile he'd ever witnessed. It just looked so *fake.* Especially after her scolding. Everyone saw her ordering him around. Did Joanne think their patrons were foolish?

"Enjoy the game!" She waved as collective cheers came from the nearby bleachers. Their stand was hitched beside it. She noticed Xavier's stares and snapped her fingers. "You have a long line in front of you," she hissed aggressively.

Xavier exchanged looks with a local seamstress, who seemed unimpressed. He laughed awkwardly. "She cares a lot about getting work done." He gave the woman her drink. "Enjoy the game, Ms. Patsy."

"I will, Xavier," she side-eyed Joanne, who ran for some pastries in the back. The young woman retrieved five cookies, then wrapped them in foil. "And tell Ms. Frosty over there to give you a break," Ms. Patsy left with a limp.

He only laughed. *Ah, Joanne.* For now, she was steely, but soon, he'd smooth out her rough edges. "Someone help Ms. Patsy to her seat," he called to two teenagers leaving the hot dog stand. "Thanks, guys," he smiled at the next customer. "Hello, Miss. What can I get for you today?"

It was a girl wearing a Sweetgum jersey, just a size too big. Her hair was in braids wrapped in a bun. On her face was the brightest smile he'd seen a person wear. "Oh, you know. Just two coffees for me and my boo." She held the counter's edge and then turned her head toward Joanne's line. "Jo! Jo!" she stage-whispered.

Xavier scratched his head while buyers watched the field. Though Joanne stressed quick service, no one seemed that concerned with his pacing. They'd take in their game wherever they stood. "Would you prefer if Joanne served you?" he asked with a tilted head.

Joanne finally faced the bouncing young woman, and to Xavier's stun, her smile rivaled the girl's in brightness. From her lips to her eyes radiated bliss. *Was this Joanne the same one he'd worked with?* "Hey, Nev. How's the game going?" she asked, handing out cookies. The next customer came forward.

Nev? Xavier listened incredulously to their conversation. Joanne must have really hated him and Peachwood. She'd never expressed such pure happiness while here. He saw how a few waiting customers looked away from the match. They stared as Joanne giggled with 'Nev,' exuding the warmth she'd yet to show them. He couldn't blame them for staring. Like he'd said, Joanne morphed from who they'd been dealing with. He felt kind of hurt, actually. That and smitten. Happiness was a good look for her.

"Is this him?" 'Nev' shielded her lips with a hand to whisper. Of course, Xavier heard every word, now becoming curious. Was she referring to him?

Joanne visibly blanched, then mouthed something. He couldn't tell what it was, but this Nev character laid off. Not before teasing Joanne, by mouthing words of her own. Again, Xavier didn't catch them. He noticed her snickering when facing him again. "Yeah, I'll have two coffees and two cookies, please. Got a kid with me," she tapped her thumbs in wait.

Xavier found himself pondering on what they might have whispered. "Coming right up." Under the top counter was a low table where Joanne left napkins. He shot a look at her.

Once again, Joanne's forced smile returned. She dealt with customers robotically, like before. Xavier wished for her welcoming aura to come back, but it seemed she reserved it for friends. *Doesn't she love her customers, though?* Or were they only strangers in Joanne's eyes? Sources of cash for business? Whatever it was, it needed to change. His fellow Peachwood Grovers just witnessed her switch up. So far, those who'd noticed looked disgruntled. *This just won't do.*

They were in the last few minutes of the fourth quarter of the game. Not a soul could look away as both teams scrambled like maniacs. With tied scores, the teams were neck in neck. It was anyone's game, really. Fans roared as the football sailed across the field. At last, it landed right in Sweetgum's grasp, channeling a mad sprint from its holder. An insane chase followed where Peachwood players raced to tackle him. A captivating sight this was. Xavier couldn't look away.

Their coffee supply had run dry just minutes ago. When the last customer hurried to his bench, Joanne started cleaning. Xavier promised he'd help soon, but for now, this game held him hostage. He leaned on the counter to watch, a towel on his shoulder. He whistled. A player had just leaped over four bodies who'd fallen before him. Yes, Peachwood seized the ball. "Let's go!"

Joanne settled beside him, closing a lunch bag of thermostats. "Enjoying the game?" she grunted. She put the bag on the counter and asked him to zip it. Xavier hadn't seen her struggling.

"Sorry, Ms. Richards. It's just insane how many tricks players pull when their lives are on the line." He easily closed the bag for her. "Let me help with folding some towels." He dragged the one he had off his shoulder. "Starting with this one," Xavier winked, then went to the back. He'd seen games like that one before. Both teams were too good. They'd end in a tie.

Joanne helped out by piling napkins into a plastic box. She squatted to do so. They'd left many boxes on ground level. "You sure do know the people here."

Xavier dusted a towel stained with coffee. He folded it anyway and placed it in the 'soiled towel' bag over Joanne. She lifted her napkin box to work at his level, her shoulder touching his. "Peach-wood people or football lovers?" He knew what she meant. Xavier just liked messing with her.

She rolled her eyes. "Peachwood residents. I've seen you greet every single person at the shop by name and now it's the same here. Like you're the mayor or something," Joanne frowned. "Actually, not the mayor, because mayors don't take the time to know people's names like you do." She held the counter with one hand. "What? Were you at everyone's christening? Are you the collective god-father of Peachwood?"

What a hilarious concept! "I didn't know you had a sense of humor," he laughed.

Joanne's deep brown eyes narrowed. "A better one than you, I'm sure. Never heard a joke of yours land since we met." She got back to work, now packing the remaining empty cups.

"Ouch," Xavier touched his chest. She hid a tiny smirk, which he loved on her face. This was good. Talking to Joanne with no barriers felt nice. Familiar even. *She still has a million walls up, though.* He'd only seen her unbarricaded while addressing her friend. He wanted that more often. In her business especially. *I always get what I want.* A several-step-plan, took form in his mind. "We probably just have different senses of humor." He folded another towel. "But back to my relationship with Peachwood. I just love this town. It's where I grew up, and the people here have been there for me in my darkest hours."

Joanne didn't speak for a while. "I see."

Xavier left his past behind to make eye contact. "I feel like I owe it to them to be as involved as possible. I'm in almost every club there is in town," he chuckled sheepishly. "But I like it. Being in so many clubs and on varying committees is why I know people's names. I also vet the businesses moving in here. I just want to see Peachwood thrive, you know?" he saw her brow arching.

"Vet?" Joanne leaned her elbow on the counter. "So that's what's going on with Roasted Beans. Did someone assign you this role, or are you some sort of big shot?" her eyes held skepticism.

Cold sweat saturated his pores. It drained down his back, soaking Xavier's shirt. She was getting too close to an area he didn't want to touch just yet. "No. It's just something I do. I'm just an ordinary guy who wants the best for Peachwood," he remembered his visit to Roasted Beans' main branch in Sweetgum, then his first encounter with Joanne. Before his interview, she'd stolen his breath. "This is just how I am."

"Because you're some kind of business expert? Do other people know that you do this?" She stopped her task to drop more questions on Xavier. "Wait, are you part of some secret society here or something? Is this just a Peachwood thing?" She inched closer.

Xavier didn't mean to cause such distrust. "No, no, this is just a me thing. There's no one else involved. Like I said, it's my way to give back."

Joanne seemed pensive. As chants and cheers bombarded them, she poked Xavier's chest. "So you mean to tell me that with every business in Peachwood, you become their manager and try to take over?" Her perplexity was undeniable. "You must be quite the busy man," she said as she detached her finger.

Xavier got tingles where she touched. "Not exactly. Let's say that when I do my overseeing, I sort of take on different approaches. With Roasted Beans, I was more on." He struggled to cover his tracks. Why did he say that? Knowing Joanne, she might look into him. What would she think once she found out?

Joanne squinted, twisting her plump, glossed lips. "But you just said you're like this with everyone." She crossed her arms with a bent neck. "So, you're *not* like this with everyone and you just enjoy being close to my business specifically? Is it because I seem hopeless in your eyes?" She advanced, forcing him to back up.

Xavier allowed her to back him into one of the bordering counters. He held the edge of it with both hands, staring down at her. Their tent lights reflected in her pupils like tiny stars. She looked majestic. Like a fairy of sorts. *An angry fairy.* "Of course not. Haven't I already voiced how I feel about you? In that... in that..." he never stammered, but she snatched his words right from his brain.

"In that what?"

"In that, I see you as a capable businesswoman. Trust me, Joanne." He slapped a quick lie together with hopes of extinguishing this interrogation. "I've been the manager of at least two other businesses while they were coming up. I just decided to be like this with Roasted Beans because it's been a while." He propped himself up by sitting on the counter.

She left him alone, now standing akimbo. "You're... a *horrible* liar."

Xavier grabbed his chest, mouth agape. "I'm telling the truth," he laughed. "Why don't you believe me?"

"Because everything you say sounds ridiculous, but whatever." She went back to packing. "I guess I should give you my thanks," Joanne said as she bowed melodramatically. "Thank you, oh great overseer of Peachwood, for inspecting my business and allowing me to serve your loyal subjects." She straightened herself with a stone-cold face. "Bet you like that, huh?"

Xavier did like it when she made fun of him. "You know," he hopped off the counter, landing on his feet. He stepped beside her. "I think that doing comedy part-time would suit you pretty well,

Joanne. You're a lot funnier than you let on." He picked up a half-folded towel, then tapped her shoulder. "What do you say?"

Joanne shrugged him off. "I'd say I have too many obligations for such a thing but that I am sincerely complimented." She batted her everlasting lashes.

A rush went through him just then. "All right," she may have rejected his touch, but Xavier would not hold that against her. He was a touchy-feely kind of guy, but she clearly wasn't like that. It didn't mean loosening her up was impossible. No matter what, Xavier would not back down. Before Joanne knew it, she'd treat every customer like 'Nev.' As if they were family.

CHAPTER ELEVEN

$\mathcal{J}$oanne blew out the heaviest sigh she'd ever released that Monday morning.

Beside her laptop were scattered documents. Some spread across her keys. On the screen was a chart she'd created on 'Chart Wizard.' A very detailed chart containing discouraging information. She listened to the pitter-patter of raindrops through her window, then spun her chair.

Outside was gray; dulling her already dull view of an empty alley. She focused as rain slid down her window, telling her to sink. Sink deep in her seat and forget work for today. October was almost through, but she hadn't met her goals. Why keep trying, right? *No.* Joanne fought her dismal thought pattern. Gloomy days often messed up her mood, but she'd learned to combat them. Only the weak stayed down when pushed. True warriors pushed back. That was Joanne's way.

She took a deep breath with her eyes gently closed. *Just need to try something new. By December, I'll have my desired numbers.* This was only a setback. Nothing more, nothing less.

"Knock, knock," Xavier called out from behind her door.

Joanne had half a mind to shoo him off. She usually recuperated alone. The presence of another would mess with her flow. "He's the manager," she grumbled. He might have important information to relay.

Reluctantly, she spun forward. "Come in." She reached for her coffee behind her laptop for a sip.

In came Xavier, dressed up in uniform. Some flour on his collar caught her eye. "Good morning, Ms. Richards. Just wanted to inform you..." He clicked her door closed on his way to her desk. "That we're a bit low on flour, so I just placed an order for a hundred pounds." he clasped his hands, appearing pleased for a reason she didn't know.

Yet another sigh flew from her mouth. "Okay. No problem. Thanks." Joanne rolled closer to her desk. She took two gulps of coffee, then put down her cup. "Is that all?" Today, she wore a black pants suit rather than the uniform. Her plan was to leave the manual work to Xavier. Some unanswered emails required her attention.

Xavier hooked his thumbs in his pockets. "Yes, but..." his brows knitted in what looked like worry. "Is everything all right?" he inspected her cluttered desk inquisitively.

Joanne chewed her inner lip, re-reading her screen charts. More than anything, she desired solitude. Alone-time to reflect on this data. She eyed Xavier's expression of anticipation, then rubbed her left brow. Sending him off would be senseless. This man was the manager. She couldn't let her own petty irritation cause her to withhold valuable information from him. Either way, he'd find out. So why not share now?

She grunted and caressed her loose hair. "I'd anticipated higher sales by now. If we continue on this trajectory, we won't meet the goals I set for December," her voice hitched while explaining. "I'm sorry. I'm just trying to think of solutions to this problem. November will be on us in no time, and yet..." She cupped her cheeks with two hands, "We have a full house every morning, but the rest of the day is just in no way comparable. I don't know." Joanne's elbows hit the table, supporting her head.

Xavier hummed, then grabbed his lower chin. "Hmm..." he yanked out a chair in front of her, then sat. "So that's it, huh?" he murmured.

Joanne rolled herself closer, lifting some stapled files. "It's all here," she handed one over. "I know we've just opened and sometimes new businesses can be slow, but so far, what I put into opening doesn't come *close* to our profits." She adjusted her loose strands of hair by flattening them with a palm. "I didn't say this to worry you, though. It's just—"

"Oh, I'm not worried," Xavier paged through the document. He closed it and set it down behind Joanne's laptop. "And I'm not too surprised either."

These words boiled Joanne's blood. "What?" she suddenly recalled his prior lectures and suggestions. "I get it," she crossed her sleeved arms. "You think numbers are down because I thwarted your plans," an angered laugh left her mouth. "You can't be serious right now. I mean, come on. Who's to say that this outcome could have been prevented if we'd done things your way?"

"Woah, woah, Ms. Richards," he said hastily. "I by no means was about to say 'I told you so,'" She saw softness behind his humored eyes. Though Joanne hated being laughed at, she did find his behavior reassuring. His mannerisms reminded her of a friend calming her down. "After all, if Roasted Beans isn't doing well, it's sad news for me, too. We're in this together, remember?"

Joanne clicked her manicured fingernails against the desk. "Together..." she repeated grudgingly. She'd subtracted him from the equation time and time again. In her eyes, this was *her* business, so *her* responsibility. But he always re-added himself when she removed him. She'd at first chalked it up to Xavier being a jerk, but maybe he truly *did* care.

The man linked his fingers on the table. "Look, we can improve things. Don't lose heart," he crossed one leg over the other. "The only reason our numbers aren't where you want them is because you've opened in a town that doesn't know you." He poked the left side of his skull. "Remember, back in Sweetgum, everyone was familiar with who you were. I'm right, aren't I? People over there knew your family and yourself?"

Joanne saw exactly where this would go. "Yes. And Peachwood isn't Sweetgum and yada, yada, yada," she'd finish his sentence on his behalf. "Is that what you're saying? That folks here in Peachwood aren't like folks in Sweetgum?" She picked up her drink again. "If so, then I've already heard you say this a million times."

"No, listen," he continued gently. Xavier beat a finger on her desk. "What I'm saying is that, *of course,* your branches in Sweetgum would thrive immediately. Everyone over there saw you as their own. They knew your family and watched you grow up, so obviously, when you opened a café, they were all eager to help out," he said. "When it boils right down to it, Peachwood, *is* a lot like Sweetgum in that people like supporting their community members. And unfortunately..." His shoulders rose, then dropped before he brushed a hand through his twisted hair. "You're not one of them here, Joanne."

Joanne's mind opened to what he was saying. "Therefore?" she prompted.

That annoying smile she'd gotten used to appeared on his full lips. "Therefore, you need to let the people know you," he parted his hands. "Establish a relationship with them, build community so they'd spend their extra dollars here instead of at the diner."

"So what? You want me joining community clubs like you? Should I learn everyone's names and call them by it?" she put her arms on the desk. "If Roasted Beans was that well-known brand that's opened branches across the country, Peachwood Grovers wouldn't give two hoots if I knew their names," she laughed in frustration, stroking her forehead. "Aren't I correct?"

He gave a negative response. "People here don't like blood-sucking corporations. How many times do I have to say what we value? Warmth, honesty, friendliness. Like how you treated Nev. They want to feel like your friend, Joanne. How many big-name establishments have you seen here since moving?" he said, leaning back.

Now that Joanne thought of it, she couldn't name any. "Wow… so have all brand-name businesses failed here in Peachwood? You guys are picky."

Xavier raised his chin. "If you aren't for the people, we aren't for you." He sat forward. "Anyway, I'm requesting permission to enact a few ideas. Ideas that will surely turn business around if you'll allow them. I promise. Just let me work my magic, Ms. Richards? I… I know how we can change things for the better. All I need is your permission to do so."

She listened to his earnestness while thinking. *I don't know*, he'd made some great points, and she really did want positive changes. But to give up control? To relinquish her authoritative position? She bit her lip. The very thought made her sick. For as long as she could remember, she'd been in charge. In charge of her goals, dreams, and aspirations. She trusted herself over others and loved holding the wheel. Especially when it came to her business. But now, holding the wheel seemed to have restricted her. The numbers didn't lie. "Well…" she hadn't known him long, but one thing was undeniable. He cared about Roasted Beans. Even her friends agreed. Most managers would not be so opinionated, but he was. He clearly wanted its success more than anything. Otherwise, he might have quit after all her warnings. "Okay, fine."

"Yes!" Xavier hopped from his chair, pumping a fist in the air. "Thank you so much. I promise that better days are ahead. You won't be disappointed!" He ran right out while singing merrily.

Joanne slumped when he left. Just *talking* to him was exhausting. "But, wait!" She needed some ground rules laid first. Knowing Xavier, he'd relocate if boundaries weren't set. "Xavier!" She ran from her seat to catch up to him.

CHAPTER TWELVE

Xavier reflected back to the note taped to his door a few days ago that gave him license to put all his plans into place:

> I need to check up on things back in Sweetgum. Watch the shop while I'm gone. Please just make sure business runs smoothly. You can do that, can't you?

He carried trays of fresh bagels from the kitchen and watched as his employees multitasked to get things done. They had a packed line in their redesigned lobby. He'd spent the weekend shifting chairs and tables to get that true communal spirit theme. The new rounded tables held more patrons than their square counterparts. He admired how groups took seats in large numbers.

"Can I get some more whipped cream in my Mr. Antoine special?" a carpenter named Gregory dinged the counter bell that afternoon.

This lunch hour saw lawyers from the downtown firm, construction workers, and high schoolers. Each seemed appreciative of Roasted Beans' new seating arrangement. Normally, only four customers fit in one booth at once, but now, up to seven could gather. "I'll get you that whipped cream, Greg. Just hang on." He set the bagels where they belonged before lifting a can of whipped cream and spraying some into Greg's mug; he saluted the carpenter. "Enjoy."

Greg smiled under his mustache. "I think I will. No wonder Mr. Antoine likes these so much. This latte is phenomenal," he said as he sauntered off contentedly.

"So glad you like it," Xavier said. Both cashiers had their hands full with customers. He'd only implemented changes on Monday, but business already took a turn. On top of the lobby's new layout, Xavier also relocated their community bulletin board and added two more menu boards. He loved watching patrons read through their specials while entering. People loved his adjustments and seemed to spread the word. Another great change was his 'Free Toppings Tuesdays' idea. With it being Tuesday, they'd had customers requesting chocolate sprinkles on desserts and coffees all day. Parents brought their kids just for the feature. Cookies and donuts were flying off the shelves!

"Good job so far, guys. Let's keep things flowing smoothly like a river," he clapped for the busy workers. Xavier raised a portion of the counter and slipped out to check on customers.

"Xavier!" A young lady with her friends came in and sat by the window.

Xavier grinned. "Sheela! What's going on?" He walked over to greet her. "How are you ladies doing? Wow, Margret, I love the hair. You all look amazing." He wiped frosting from his apron while they accepted his compliments.

Sheela patted her short hair, then lifted her cup. "First of all, we're all loving what you've done to this place, and second," she slushed her drink around her mug. "Is there any chance you give refills on the house?" She cracked a smile before snickering. "I'm kidding," her friends laughed as well.

"Haha. You always were a joker," he said as he noticed the empty mugs of her besties. "Hmm, but having a free refill day isn't so much of a bad idea. Do you ladies think people would like that?"

"Yes!" They nodded excitedly. "I'd come here three times a day if you did that. Although, you might cause some addiction if you made refills unlimited," Margret put a hand to her mouth, pretending her words were secret. She'd projected her voice to be heard since countless conversations rattled around them. Not a booth was empty this fine afternoon. After seeing Xavier's new design, coming here for lunch seemed appealing to the masses. Or more like coming for dessert *after* lunch.

Xavier had to agree. "Right. I'd specify how many are allowed. I'd say just one free refill per customer." They seemed satisfied with that. "Great. So, Refill Wednesdays are *on*. I'll talk to the staff about it. Oh, and the owner, too." He started backing up. "Are you guys enjoying your donuts?"

Sheela gave a thumbs up. "It's amazing, but where *is* that owner of yours? The pretty girl who always looks serious."

He came back with eyes toward the window. Outside seemed packed with marching pedestrians. He wished they'd come in. Today, Roasted Beans had some great vibes. He'd never been so laid back. "Joanne?" he pocketed his hands. "She's over at Sweetgum, overseeing some business."

"Oh yes, she's from Sweetgum. Why did she open here in Peachwood, of all places?" Asked a lady with her back to the window. She wiped her mouth of frosting.

He forgot that not everyone knew Joanne's story. "She has branches in Sweetgum. There are about three cafés like this one over there. Her branch here is simply her idea of expanding. It's great because she's really young but already has a successful chain of coffee shops," bringing up Joanne reminded Xavier of his drastic design changes. Sure, their customers liked it, but what about the boss? Rejecting his input was practically in Joanne's DNA. This time around, she'd given him the 'OK' to go wild, but that didn't mean she'd approve. *I already spent so much money.* He scratched his face.

"Impressive," Sheela and her friends agreed. "I didn't know there were branches in Sweetgum," she said softly. "So, she left things to you while she's over there?"

"It's so funny how he's dressed in uniform, like an ordinary person. Xavier, you're this town's pride." They sang his praises with elation.

Xavier acted bashful on purpose. "Sometimes, to achieve our goals, we have to get down and dirty. This is me doing that."

Sheela's neck bent to the left. "And what's your goal for this café, and why do you care so much about it?" she questioned teasingly. Her smirk made it clear what she assumed. "Or is it not so much about the café and more something else?"

Xavier got hot flashes at their prying. "Come on, ladies. You know how much I love supporting small businesses." A bead of sweat raced down his forehead. "When it comes to businesses in Peachwood, I want them to perform optimally. You know why?" he stepped backward. "Because our people deserve A plus service. That's all that's happening here," he ended with a thumbs up.

Sheela's furrowed brows showed he hadn't convinced her. "Okay, Xavier. If that's all there is to it, then congrats. You're doing amazing. I'm sure your boss will love what you've done," she said as she faced her friends, who snickered.

"I sure hope she does," Xavier muttered, walking back to the counter. He was just lifting the moveable portion when a barrister spoke. The boy carried two cups bearing names.

"Sir, was Ms. Richards supposed to come back today?" he asked, putting down the coffee. "Caitlin and John! Your orders are up!"

Xavier quietly stood beside him, his back to the dining room. "She is," he said. "But probably later," bakers traveled in and out of the bakery with steaming hot treats. All this constant motion made room for accidents. He almost witnessed one between a server and a chef. "Take it easy, guys! We want fast service, but not at our own expense. The customers aren't going anywhere," he said, clapping three times. "Why do you ask?"

Caitlin and John said their thanks after collecting their drinks. "Enjoy," the barrister aimed a chin ahead. "Sorry, Sir. That lady just reminds me of her, but I doubt that it is. Ms. Richards doesn't sit around unless it's to work." He glided back to his post, accepting another labeled cup from his coworker. A small group of customers waited for their drinks. Their chit-chatting told Xavier they hadn't grown disgruntled. Not one of them appeared impatient. A friendly environment did improve customer satisfaction.

"What?" Xavier just registered the boy's observation. He searched for what the youngster described. *Wait,* there. Someone *did* sit alone up ahead in a corner. Her seat had been pulled from a table at her left. No one appeared aware of her distress. *Joanne?* The black blazer and electric blue undershirt matched her style, but apart from that, nothing else was synonymous. *Wait, the hair, too.* He recognized the looping brown curls. Could it be? This person hung their head, hands smothering their face, very out of character for Joanne. He always carded her as one who hid her emotions. Joanne would never sit and sulk in the open.

Unless... something wasn't right.

Instantly, Xavier returned to the lobby. He set eyes on his boss and saw nothing else. This could mean one of two things. Joanne either saw his 'improvements' and lost her mind from disapproval or hadn't had a good visit back home. He doubted the latter, so chose the first. How awful? He'd driven her to insanity. Perhaps a nice chat would help. Xavier put together an argument about why these changes were good. They'd seen their first lunch hour rush yesterday. Today marked their second. These milestones were cause for celebration. Once Xavier filled her in on this, Joanne would simmer down. Or at least, he hoped so. *Worst-case scenario, I lose my job.* And with that, his chances.

"Hey," Xavier rubbed the back of his neck, standing in the corner. Though Joanne sat before him, this sensation of isolation crept in. Everyone seemed farther than they were. This corner, himself, and Joanne were all he saw. Her single red chair looked small and lonely. "Is everything okay, boss?"

Joanne's handbag sat on the ground. She'd flung it beside her chair. He could tell based on her scattered belongings. Again, very out of character for her. His brain split in two. Half refused to believe this was his boss, while the other half knew for sure. He needed to see her face to be convinced.

No reply.

As customers went in and out with time ticking by, Xavier squatted. "Joanne, if this is you, nod twice." Apart from the soft grunts, this woman was silent. Her behavior garnered stares. He didn't help by looking at her so anxiously.

Finally, a reaction was given. She dropped her hands, revealing bulging eyes and a trembling jaw. Her face shot in every direction but his, searching in disbelief. Whatever she was looking for, Xavier could not find. "Joanne?" Yes, this woman was certainly his grouchy boss, but not the boss he'd come to know. This Joanne didn't look self-assured or stubborn. And she surely wasn't confident. Whatever confidence she'd had must have vanquished. He saw no trace of it.

"Mr. Antoine Special, Dan's Delight… t—tables…" he heard the panic in her words. Joanne's voice quivered like a sheet in a blizzard, resembling a child more than an authoritative adult. "Why is it… why did it…"

Xavier's chest seized up. She hated it. Her behavior was directly linked to the Roasted Beans' makeover. "Ms. Richards, look. I know I've modified a lot, but you need to understand that—" he attempted an explanation, but her mind seemed elsewhere. Anywhere but present.

Joanne fixed her gaze on something past Xavier. He twisted himself to see, but couldn't make a connection between her eyes and anything behind him. This led Xavier to conclude she stared into space, further increasing his apprehension. She looked so unfocused and terrified, wild even. He hadn't meant to hurt her. All Xavier wanted was Joanne's satisfaction. To improve her business. But in chasing this, he'd shaken her wellbeing. "Ms. Richards, can you hear me? Ms. Richards, nod twice if you hear me."

She never broke away from staring, and now her breathing became erratic. It started as deep inhales but soon became shallow. So shallow that Xavier feared she'd pass out. Was she having a panic attack? He grabbed her shoulders as patrons turned from their beverages. "Ms. Richards, feel me. Feel my hands on your shoulders. Look at my face and try to stay with me. Look into my eyes. What color are my eyes?" He had a hard time talking quietly. Xavier didn't want more attention drawn to this, but feared it was too late.

"Is she okay?" someone asked behind him.

He faked a smile at the man. "Yes, Will. She just needs me to keep her grounded. Try not to stare too much. It'll make her worse." His throat went dry as he continued assisting her. "Let's go to your office. I think we should go."

Joanne's breathing steadied itself, and her dark eyes rose with Xavier. He prayed that she'd come back to him but realized this was wishful thinking. Joanne may have breathed better, but her emotions had not subsided. They just took a new form.

CHAPTER THIRTEEN

Order, predictability, control. From a very young age, these elements had been pounded into Joanne's psyche. Her upbringing labeled them the ingredients for stability. Back home, down to the smallest of utensils had to be arranged a particular way. Otherwise, all hell would break loose. Because of this, she'd associated stringency with ideality. One could regard her case as a means to pity her, but Joanne had always used her upbringing as a guideline. A way to ensure that life went exactly as she wanted. Joanne took life by the reins and steered it where she believed she should go. If there was one thing she'd picked up, it was that being in charge meant life would bend to her will. Would go where she ordered it because she said so. Who wouldn't want complete command over their destiny? Anyone 'going with the flow' was flippant and destined for mediocrity. But not Joanne. She'd always believed in her outlook and approach because it worked. It hadn't failed her as long as she'd lived. And she truly believed that it wouldn't.

That was, until now.

If only she'd split herself evenly. If she'd dedicated time to supervising both branches in equal amounts, then the catastrophe at

Sweetgum's main branch wouldn't have come about. Her constant meddling in Peachwood's operations made Joanne neglectful. Now, she needed to replace a barrister for theft. Theft of all things! She'd had a chat with the teen behind the missing tips and toppings this morning. Joanne believed in second chances and wanted to spare one to the teen, but their crime's reasoning offended her. There was no sad sob story or trials at home. The kid confessed to stealing because they got 'bored' and believed they'd get away with it. That revelation *burned.* She'd handpicked every one of her employees. Usually, they wound up being top-tier. How could she have missed such a bad egg? These were questions she'd asked while driving back to Peachwood. She'd concluded that her absence was what led this on. If only she'd let Peachwood go.

After thinking it through longer, Joanne realized something. By no means was her outlook wrong. That disaster proved it more correct than ever. Every one of her projects required close supervision. She'd never look away again. Without her inspection, everything would spiral, including Joanne herself.

She'd fought tooth and nail with her thoughts to keep them at bay. Joanne had wanted a fresh mind while checking in on Peachwood. From outside, business had looked good. People had been coming in and leaving at lunch hour, something she wasn't used to. She'd wanted to accept this as a breath of fresh air, but after going in, the changes gave her whiplash.

New menu boards, foreign chairs, strange new drinks. She hadn't approved of anything called a 'Dan's Delight'. What was that? Again, her questions came swirling like a twister. Joanne hadn't recognized her own café. For a while, she'd wondered if she'd mixed hers up with another. Questioning her sanity made things worse. It got so bad, that Joanne had run outside to crosscheck. The 'Roasted Beans Coffee Spot' logo hadn't helped. Confirming that her business had changed drastically sent her spinning. She would have lost balance if she hadn't grabbed a seat. At that point, Joanne had needed a break. She'd gotten an immediate headache that pulsed through her brain, eyes, and skull. Panicking so obviously was new to her adult life. Joanne had not known what to do, but Xavier's appearance aggravated her condition.

At first, none of his talking came through. Only her rapid breaths were heard, squeaking through her eardrums. It was only when he touched her that she returned to reality. *Let's go to your office.* The idea made her pause.

Xavier didn't part eyes from her. He gripped her knee like a life-line, watching Joanne cautiously.

She had so much to say. So much to tell him for going over-board, but right now, she harbored no anger. No malice or fury came forth. Yes, her pathetic state was partially his fault, but Joanne wasn't annoyed. She'd been stretched too thin and was now worn out. Worn right to the bone. Why? This was her café. Her bread and butter that *she* worked hard on. Yet still, he continuously interfered. Was he not aware of subtility? Couldn't he make gradual adjust-ments? What was this? Why did Xavier *insist* on bulldozing what she'd established? "You—" Joanne stopped when a hard sob popped out of her. It stirred her body, which shook with distress. More and more sobs came after, lurching her forward. *No.* How humiliating!

"Joanne," Xavier breathed, looking sorry.

Joanne ignored every staring eye to shield herself with trembling hands. Behind them she bawled. Why this and why now? She wanted to hide, to curl up but at her age, she shouldn't. "No," she whimpered.

"All right. We have to go." Xavier pulled her up with an arm around her body. He walked Joanne away, letting her hide in his chest. She wanted to reject him but was too embarrassed. So, for once, she behaved herself and buried her face in his uniform, swal-lowing his heavenly cologne.

～

SEEING her office just how she left it was a blessing. Her wobbly legs gave way by the door. She yearned for her large leather seat but simply couldn't reach it. Xavier swaddled her like an incapable child when she lost control of her muscles. He half carried her to one of the waiting chairs by her desk. She'd request he bring her to the desk, but felt too inept to do so. Joanne always overcame stressful situations. She didn't understand what this meant. To break down so colossally with so many witnesses wasn't like her.

"There we go," the café manager spun the chair so it faced the main door. The main door that he'd shut after escorting her inside. "Want some water?" Xavier got his handkerchief. He handed it to Joanne, then backed away. "Did you eat anything? Try looking outside for a bit. I'll get you some water. Just don't move, okay? I think you had a panic attack." He left in a state, shaken and anxious.

Joanne jumped at the *click* of her door. A noise it always made. Today, it startled her, convincing Joanne that she'd lost it. *Lost control of myself.* She gulped, counting her desk files. Tracking numbers always calmed her down. When she'd left, there were five folders stacked in all. Her distance made counting a task, but she tried anyway, utilizing her finger as a method of tracing. They were arranged neatly in her straw file-holder. She stretched a tremoring finger and started. Not all was lost. Xavier hadn't touched her office.

One... two... th-three... Joanne rotated her waist to see properly. Her desk was behind her and farther than before. Why did Xavier bring the chair so far? Again with Xavier! He did this to help her, but ultimately caused pain. She hung her head in dejection, grabbing her face again. He just wanted what was best. Both when it came to Roasted Beans *and* Joanne herself. The man had gone out of his way to support her here. He could have left her in the dining room. Heck, someone else would. After everything she'd done to shut down his ideas, Joanne herself mightn't have extended a hand like he had.

She fought for reason inside her agitated brain. If Joanne

persisted in blaming Xavier and allowing him to enrage her, she just might collapse. Though his 'upgrades' were completely out of line, approaching them with ferocity wasn't good for her. Therefore, when he returned, she'd calmly apprise him of what could stay, then move forward. All she needed now was to find her voice. She was calm enough to breathe, so would surely gain her wits back. This frazzled state just would not do.

Eeer, Xavier swung her door open upon return and clicked it shut. In his free hand was a glass of water. The man let go of the doorknob and showed her a paper bag. "Do you like donuts?"

Joanne dried tears from her eyes with his hankey. It smelled like detergent. Flowery and sweet. She tried answering but was incapable. The second she opened her mouth, heavy weights dragged her downward. They strapped to her tongue, arms, and torso, rendering her speechless. Rather than opening up, Joanne rested back, sighing.

"Here," he crouched, placing the glass in her hand. "Can you hold it?"

Joanne applied pressure to secure it. She sniffed when her nose threatened to run, then jerked the water at her lips, spilling some on her top. It shocked her and disrupted what little peace she'd mustered. Again, her delirium made an appearance, convincing her she'd lost her grip on herself and everything around her.

"It's okay, look," Xavier took the glass before bringing it to her lips. "Drink. Don't worry about anything. Just sip at your own pace. I'll help you."

Joanne's eyes penetrated the ring below her cup. Water slid to her mouth, and she let it. She took two sips before pulling back. "E-enough."

Xavier held it back in surprise. He stared incredulously. "Are you okay?"

Joanne examined her cold palms, then used her blazer sleeve as a napkin, dabbing her chin. She requested the glass and drained its contents. "Thank you."

He accepted it back. "You're welcome," he said, giving her the paper bag. "Hungry?" he asked, displaying uncertain relief. He treated her like a ticking time bomb. As much as she despised it, she understood why he had to.

Reluctantly, she took the donuts and pulled one out. The delicious baked goods made her mouth water. Covered in frosting and sprinkles, she was reminded of the last time she ate. That being breakfast. Being so busy often distracted her. She didn't always find time for what mattered most: taking care of her health and wellbeing. For once, Joanne put these first by munching down the dessert. She dug in unapologetically, caring not for Xavier's presence. Slowly, her command reappeared. She'd spoken and could now eat. All she'd needed was a snack.

"You can use the napkin to wipe that off." Xavier waved at her mouth. "You have a little something there." He brushed a thumb by his lip.

Joanne cleaned her face and hands. She crushed the donuts' packaging with an exhale. She couldn't pinpoint whether she was satisfied or exhausted. Whatever it was made her sleepy. Like she'd blown out her last reserves of energy. Four hours of the day remained. Joanne couldn't sit around because of drowsiness.

Yet, she made no move to address Xavier's actions. They both sat quietly, staring. She at him because she needed motivation to speak, and he at her because… well Joanne didn't know. He seemed less worried, but his eyes contained a hidden emotion. Joanne wasn't sure what it meant.

"Can I share something with you?" he asked.

CHAPTER FOURTEEN

othing on earth could have prepared him for Joanne's outburst. Sure, he'd clocked how critically she deemed control, but something deeper had to be at play. Whatever psychological reason there was for Joanne's autocratic nature, he'd try to break down. While Xavier could acknowledge her struggles, he also saw their limitations. Abiding by such a restricting mindset might harm her in the long run. He hoped she'd allow him to give his input.

Joanne wiped her nose with the napkin he'd given her. "Share something?" she was hoarse.

Xavier grunted, standing straight. He put his hands on his hips, then bent himself backwards. "Yes. If you're open to listening." The tear stains under her eyes made his heart ache.

His boss sat back with her elbow on the chair arm. She deflated visibly, then said a short, "Yes."

"Back when I was in high school, I was a football player." He went over to her desk and leaned against it. With fingers combing his scalp, he surrendered himself to distant memories. Events he'd locked away. Pain shot up his spine when he recalled them.

Her chair faced the opposite direction. To show she was listening, Joanne gave her side profile to Xavier. She squinted slightly. "Why aren't you playing now?"

He smiled. "A lot happened between then and now," he said crossing his arms across his chest. "It was honestly a roller coaster, but I'm getting sidetracked." He blew a puff of air through his mouth. "Anyway, I was really good. Star quarterback and golden boy of the team. I worked hard, scored touchdowns every game, and attracted attention from all directions," he said, visualizing himself clad in his football uniform. The signature bulky padded shoulders brought him great nostalgia. Their colors were red and white. "Agents, scouts, you name it."

"I was so good that all sorts of colleges were lining up to accept me. Everyone was so proud to know that someone from Peachwood, a town so small it's not on some maps, could garner so much recognition. In the end, I got a full football scholarship to a prestigious university, which I gladly accepted. Boy, were we excited. Not just my family but the entire town. I couldn't wait to show off my skills across the country." His arms unlinked and dropped slowly. "And show off I did." No longer could Xavier see Joanne. She'd merged with his surroundings. He focused on nothing but somehow saw everything. They started blurring as flashbacks resurfaced relentlessly. "Instantly, I became the school's top performer. MVP, captain, prodigy, they labeled me everything. I trained hard and did whatever I could to keep our team on top. At that point, talks about going pro were starting up." A trance-like presence consumed him. This was all ancient history, but in its time, so monumental. So, riveting. He'd been in his prime and very optimistic. "Again, agents and scouts came to my games showing interest. Being so young and thinking I might have a shot at making a living off something so incredible had me over the moon."

At last, he saw Joanne again. Only her and her engrossment in his story. "But then, one fateful day changed everything." He recalled the sound of helmets colliding as darkness clouded his subconscious. "Finals game against our top rivals. Rain. I remember being soaked but loving the thrill. It was incredible, but I hadn't known what was coming." He trailed two fingers down his spinal cord, shifting so Joanne caught sight. "There's a scar around here I got from surgery. You see…" he held his hands. "On that rainy day, a player twice my size tackled me so hard my spine fractured."

Joanne's breath caught. "What?"

"I know what you're thinking. How can I stand and move around today?" Xavier picked up a glass dolphin on Joanne's desk. He'd made himself comfortable sitting on it. Noticing his position, he got off. "It took a lot of work. I should have been paralyzed, but I pulled through with luck and determination." He advanced to her chair and once again stooped in front of her. "Anyway, after that happened, I couldn't play anymore. Everything. All deals, agents, screaming fans, they all disappeared in the blink of an eye," he snapped his fingers. "People turned their backs on me. After my surgery, everyone at that school saw me as the saddest case in history. My coach and lecturers expressed their regrets, but only that. I had no worth to them without my talent. It'd been a dark, *dark* time for me, but in the midst of my depression, folks from Peachwood were calling me up. Tons left town just to see how I was doing, traveling so far just to check on me. I got so many gifts and get well soon cards. They encouraged me to keep going. To fight for my ability to walk even if it was futile." He spotted glowing tears in Joanne's gorgeous eyes. "Of course, I couldn't stay over there in my condition, so I came home. When I did, I didn't get sorry looks like I'd gotten from schoolmates but instead a hero's welcome."

Sniff, Joanne swiped a stray tear racing down her face.

He wished she wouldn't cry, but if crying helped with processing, he'd allow her. It just hurt Xavier seeing Joanne sad. "They told me how proud they were of my achievements. Not only getting so far in football, but overcoming my injury. I got food on the house at so many restaurants I'd gained tons of weight. It was insane but also incredibly rewarding after being abandoned by big city folks. I don't know. Looking back, I feel like I can't thank them enough. My people. Peachwood Grovers." His eyes stung, but Xavier refused to shed tears. If both of them started spluttering, they'd never get back to work. "It's why I care so deeply about everyone here and look out for them. But that's not even why I told you all of this," Xavier poked Joanne's knee. "What I'm getting at is that I went through a *drastic* change to get where I am now. I got hurt *really* badly and had to give up football. Something I loved more than life, but it had to happen. If it didn't, I would have never come back home. And if I'd never come back home, I would've never met you."

That last part seemed to strike her as she visibly startled. But Joanne made no sound.

He got a rush; his heart pounded like a hammer. "Anyway, that's just a bit about me. I want you to know that change isn't always bad. It can be good because it leads to greener pastures in certain cases. I know it's hard for you, but that's just what I think. But if you really don't like what I did, then it's completely fine. I won't mind reverting Roasted Beans back to your preference." Looking at her made him feel warm. Why wasn't she speaking? Perhaps he'd chosen a bad time to drop his true feelings. He would have held back, but it simply flowed out of him. Thinking that a reality could have existed where their paths had not crossed was mind-boggling.

They butt heads and argued all the time, but every second was magic. He'd lie in bed smiling when envisioning her. Yes. Going pro would have doomed him to loneliness. No woman like Joanne existed. He wondered if she even noticed that he just subtly confessed his feelings for her. He feared she'd despise him for it if she did. Or maybe feel disrespected? They were boss and employee. He'd understand if Joanne could no longer work alongside him. She seemed like the type to reject work relationships. Especially those with power imbalances. He may have been older, but she had more authority.

After a while, he cut through the silence. "So, what do you think?" Xavier forced himself to ask.

She remained frozen, mute.

Xavier shifted nervously. "Is everything all right, Ms. Richards?"

Slightly, Joanne jerked her head. "Yes. I'm just… I'm just touched," she said as she placed a palm on her chest. "Thank you for opening up to me. It must have taken a lot out of you."

"It didn't since I was opening up with the intention of helping you, but you're welcome," Xavier reversed to the closed door. "You're touched, you say?" What did that mean? His brain scrambled for answers, grappling to understand.

Joanne's eyes scanned her left side. Xavier read her clearly. She was avoiding him. Her twiddling fingers and partial sways were a giveaway.

"What is it?"

At that point, she chewed her bottom lip. "There's actually a reason why I have so much trouble giving up control. At least, I think there is. Whenever I think back, it's all I can come up with. I just don't know if I should tell you."

Xavier gave her time to deliberate. She bit her tongue and went on with rocking, resembling a shy child. "If you don't want to, you don't have to. Just because I was comfortable opening up doesn't mean you have to be." Whatever she stored deep inside must have made thinking difficult. He wouldn't pry or force her, but if Joanne needed to speak, then he'd listen. "Unless you think it will help."

She became still.

CHAPTER FIFTEEN

And if I'd never come back home, I would've never met you. Did Xavier mean that? For so long, she'd built concrete walls around herself. Walls to ensure she stayed focused on business and nothing else. But without her knowledge, those walls had gone up for other reasons, too. Reasons she only now registered. *Xavier Evans.* Her handpicked manager. Joanne had feared seeing him as an option. She'd admitted to his good looks, but only that. While around him, her belly would flutter and warm, but Joanne had written this off as anger. Xavier wasn't just an insufferable manager she regretted hiring, though. He had a heart and a story. A story he told her in the name of assisting.

The second he'd expressed gratitude for meeting her, the towering walls fell and shattered. Every sensation she'd denied in his company avalanched with vigor, burying her. Her palms started sweating, her heart galloped, and she grew slightly queasy. They may have fought often, but their chemistry was undeniable, and after her business, he took second place in her thoughts. Was it possible that she'd liked him this whole time?

Joanne picked a thread on her blazer. She shrunk with her

wreathing memories running amuck inside. Because of Xavier's bravery, she now understood his devotion to Peachwood. He deserved to know what made her tick. Otherwise, they would not move forward. *It's something I've never opened up about.* Not even her friends had the details. They shared so much with one another, but Joanne had her pride. Too much of it that sometimes got in her way. Telling Xavier seemed essential, though. Currently, they needed communication.

"My dad was abusive."

Xavier's stance changed immediately. "What?" he stepped closer with a face showing remorse. "Did he hurt you? Joanne, I am *so* sorry. Just know that he's a *horrible* person who deserves the worst for—"

"No, no, he never hit me. He—he hit my mother, but not me or my little sister. Xavier, calm *down*." Joanne had never seen such pure fury. Xavier kept it cool most times. She couldn't believe how easily he'd flipped. Huffing, puffing, growling, the man did it all, and she'd only said one sentence. It warmed her heart, watching him react on her behalf.

Xavier's muscles tightened around his eyes and cheeks. He'd come forward until he loomed above her. His anger made him menacing, but it slowly subsided. He held his forehead, then rubbed a palm down his face. "Sorry," he whispered. "You grew up in an abusive household?"

Joanne saw his longing. His desperation for context. "Yes," admitting it broke her. Saying her dad was abusive wasn't as bad as calling her whole living situation the same. An abusive household felt like a sob story. A tragedy even. Something to cry over in movies. As much as Joanne despised pity, her upbringing fit 'pitiful' more than anything. "He liked having things 'just so,'" she found herself back in her childhood apartment. Its dingy wallpaper left an ache in her stomach. "Every chair needed to be under the table and our rooms spotless. No dishes in the sink and no toys in the living room when he got home." Scary memories were activated with these words. Her old man's gruff tone said the lines with her, his cheeks shaking on each word. She saw his silhouette in the swollen wooden door as he left for work. "He didn't like coming home to anything out of place. My sister and I tried our best to keep the house to his liking, but we were kids." Tears sizzled Joanne's puffy eyes.

"And kids make mistakes." It never left her. That fateful instance where she'd screwed up. Between her and her sister, it was Joanne who maintained order. Except on that day. "Usually," she looked at her hands, examining how her thumb scratched her palm. "If anything was amiss, he'd punish us by beating our mom. I think he spared us because she begged him, but it didn't hurt less watching her in pain. Sometimes, he'd hurt her just because he was angry, but the worst of them came when us kids made a mess," she hiccupped before grabbing her mouth.

Xavier's tender hand rubbed her shoulder. "Take your time."

She brushed some stray tears. "I worked really hard at cleaning just so he'd leave Mom alone, but one day after school, I came home with a headache. Mom had been at work, but that was the norm. My sister and I had dinner alone, but I couldn't muster the strength to clean. She decided to do so for me while I took a nap. By then, my headache turned into a fever that glued me to bed. I remember falling into the deepest sleep of my life. I'd been about twelve at the time." On impulse, Joanne bit her inner lip. Dark imagery she'd long since locked away brimmed like dead fish in the ocean. On every lash, she flinched like her body was assaulted. "Twelve and so, so sick," sobs racked her body, forcing her forward.

Immediately, Xavier swooped in and held her, shushing her tenderly. "It's okay, it's okay."

Joanne enjoyed his kindness and care. Behind his shirt were rock-solid abs, but his gentle hands made up for their hardness. She drew back to continue, not believing how much she let herself break down. "I was so sick that I didn't check on my sister's work.

My nap was interrupted by Dad's angry yells, and before I knew it, we were both called to the kitchen. By then, it was nighttime. I remember seeing Mom standing in front of him, begging him to let us go to our rooms, but none of her words meant a thing to him."

Xavier seemed engaged, captivated by her story. He didn't look away while arriving at her desk. There, he got a tissue from the box she left open. He inevitably seized the whole thing and handed a single piece to her, safeguarding the rest. "Why was he mad? Did your sister leave the dishes dirty?"

"She washed everything but forgot to put them away. They'd been in the drainer. Something he *hates* seeing." Anger boiled in the pits of her soul. Joanne hated recounting her worst experiences, but somehow gained comfort through sharing. Xavier's listening ear put her at ease. For the first time in her life, she wanted to open up more. "Of course, like I said, he decided to punish us by hurting our mom, and that's what he did. That time was just worse than the others. She'd wound up at the hospital but..." she halted, not wanting to revisit that.

Xavier gave her another tissue. "I'm so sorry," his eyes leaked tears of their own.

Joanne appreciated his attention. "It's okay," she dabbed the corner of her eye. "He can't hurt us anymore." It dawned on her that the room had darkened. With a quick peep, Joanne saw the sky. No longer did radiant sunrays rain onto the earth. They'd lessened significantly, leading her to believe it was evening. She checked her phone for the time.

"Why? Because you grew up and left his house?" Xavier never changed his perturbed frown. A combination of anger, worry, and compassion filled his eyes. For him to be so troubled because of her agony, truly touched Joanne. She must have meant a lot to him.

"No. My father died just as I finished my online associate's degree." She crumpled her tissues in a fist, remembering the funeral. "His death was the only reason I could open Roasted Beans in the first place. With it came cash." Her business' success brought Joanne great pride. The gloomy clouds that came with her past were overridden by its surfacing. She straightened her back and faced Xavier. "And I'm glad I put good use to something linked to him. It meant that my suffering wasn't for nothing." The grim man's creased face disintegrated from her subconscious. "In the end, he did at least one good thing for me."

CHAPTER SIXTEEN

 avier knew there had to be a reason that Joanne was so guarded, but he would have never guessed the true reason. "Suffering never serves a purpose in that sense." He wanted her to know this. "You're not deserving of rewards just because you've suffered."

Joanne seemed lost. "What?"

"You shouldn't have had to endure so much to get your shop. You deserve it because you're amazing and hardworking and should have nice things just for being you." Xavier wished she'd understand him, but it didn't seem she did. Joanne wasn't ready. "Anyway," he pulled her into another hug. Joanne rested her head on his stomach a second time. He heard her breathe out on him. "Your dad was wrong, okay? And nothing he did was your fault. He was a despicable human being," he combed her hair with his fingers.

"I know," she sighed.

They remained connected a while longer until Joanne pried herself off. "We should head out. It's almost time to close. We've stayed in here for way too long," her busy-body attitude came back full force. She stood, wiped her face, then strutted to the door.

Xavier didn't want her to leave so abruptly. "Hey, wait," he took her hand.

Joanne at first started to tug away, but paused. "We've been here too long. People have probably started assuming things." She leaned her back to the door.

Xavier closed in on her. Their faces were almost touching. "What do you think they're assuming?" he asked smoothly.

She rolled her eyes. "Why do you want me to wait? Is there something else you'd like to say?" Her snippy attitude seemed out of place with her red eyes and sniffling nose.

"Yes, actually. I want to know if you think you're okay enough to stay here. Shouldn't you leave? Recounting all of that must have drained you." He moved his hand to her wrist, holding a bracelet she wore beneath her cuff.

Joanne took a deep breath. "It was, but there's not much time left in the day." She half-smiled. "Thank you for providing a safe space for me to talk to someone." She swayed left and right again. "I think it helped."

Before he could respond, she initiated a hug, which lasted two seconds. After letting go, Xavier snatched her wrist again. "One more thing before you go." To say his heart grew ten times would be an understatement.

Those inquisitive eyes got him grinning. He wasn't sure how appropriate it was to ask, but if he didn't, he never would. "Would you mind maybe talking more about our feelings somewhere nice? You know? *Not* in a work setting?"

Joanne's eyes widened, and she squeaked out, "Our feelings? Like where?"

"Anywhere you want. At my place, at yours, over dinner, you name it."

Her hesitation made him nervous. A very foreign emotion for Xavier.

"So, you got me in my feelings just to ask me out?"

"No. Of course not. If you don't want to, you can say no. I won't ask again if you do." He held his hands up in defense.

Joanne said something softly, staring at the ceiling. "You know what?" She tapped Xavier's chest. "Why not?"

~

THAT FRIDAY EVENING was uncannily warm. As the holidays approached, it was usually windy and cold, but tonight was unexpectedly still.

Xavier opened Joanne's door, thanking God. Even now, he struggled to comprehend what had happened. Between Tuesday and tonight, he'd repeatedly asked her why she'd agreed to go out with him. But in true Joanne fashion, she never answered. The beautiful woman preferred telling him off for 'distracting' her from work. She'd come to accept his adjustments after their heart-to-heart but was still pretty stubborn in terms of everything else. It seemed their dynamic would never truly change.

"Thank you," Joanne said as she stepped onto the pavement. She wore a sleek, midnight-blue dress with delicate lace sleeves that added a hint of elegance. Paired with her chic coat, she looked effortlessly stylish. Xavier couldn't help but shower her with compliments when she first got into his car. Xavier had 'picked her up' from her office because she'd had to stay behind for an online meeting with her café managers back home, causing the need to get dressed in her office.

Xavier closed her door and nodded towards the restaurant. Nestled in a secluded area of Peachwood, Chante de Cuisine was the town's premier and most exclusive dining venue . A red carpet rolled out towards the entrance, with uniformed guards stationed at the door. Another couple had just made their entrance ahead of them. Despite the glittering night, Xavier couldn't help but notice the calmness enveloping the place. The restaurant's spot gave Peachwood a serene ambiance. He smirked, thinking that just a few blocks away on Main Street, a crowd of young revelers were probably tearing it up at some nightclub.

"Welcome to Peachwood's finest," Xavier said, guiding Joanne into the warmth of the restaurant. The expansive dining hall stretched out before them, filled with elegantly dressed patrons enjoying lavish drinks and sharing mirthful conversations. "Hope this isn't too over the top for a first date," he said, casting a glance her way, eager to gauge her response. Peachwood might have been a small town, but several of its residents were surprisingly wealthy. Himself, included.

Joanne's eyes widened in awe. "This is amazing. Just look at that chandelier!" she exclaimed, her gaze fixated on the glimmering lights overhead. "You never struck me as someone who'd enjoy high-end places. How did you come across this gem?"

Xavier mockingly placed a hand over his heart, pretending to be wounded. As a waiter approached to lead them to their table, he extended an arm for Joanne, which she gracefully accepted. "I have a few tricks up my sleeve," he replied with a sly grin, especially when she quirked an eyebrow in response.

"Xavier!" someone called from the sea of dining patrons.

Xavier froze with Joanne, recognizing the voice. Slowly, he searched for its source until finding it nearby. "Mr. Jones?" Beside their intended table was a long, grand one, reminiscent of what you'd find in a castle's banquet hall. To Xavier's dismay, not only was Mr. Jones seated there, but several other familiar faces as well. *Oh no.*

"Your table," the waiter indicated, pointing to an elegantly set round table covered in pristine cloth. The plates were graced with napkins intricately folded into the shape of cranes. The two designated seats for them were placed opposite each other. In the center of the table stood a slender blue candle.

As Joanne gracefully settled into her seat, she looked around, clearly impressed. "Wow. Looks amazing," she remarked while the waiter lit the centerpiece candle, its flame casting a soft glow and filling the air with a calming scent of lavender. Xavier was momentarily lost in thought, and her voice brought him back. "Xavier, aren't you going to sit?"

Before he could respond, her attention shifted, and she leaned in with a hint of recognition. Clutching the menu in her hand, she said, "Hey wait, that's the real estate agent who sold me the post office. You know him?"

Joanne's inquisitive tone snapped Xavier back to the moment. Adjusting his suit self-consciously, he cleared his throat. "Yes, I do," he acknowledged, casting a smile towards Mr. Jones, Eddie, and the others seated at the long table. It dawned on him that tonight was likely the annual Sky High Real Estate staff dinner. He silently hoped they'd remain engrossed in their own gathering and not drift too close to his table. If Joanne heard the truth from anyone else but him, it might shatter any trust she had in him.

Settling into his chair across from Joanne, Xavier attempted to keep his composure. "I know pretty much everyone around Peachwood. That man's just one of many I've crossed paths with over the years," he said, taking a moment to inhale the soothing aroma of the candle. "In fact, I know most of the folks at his table," he added. The soft strains of symphonic music played overhead, but it did little to alleviate his rising unease. Deciding he needed something to take the edge off, he signaled for a drink.

"Anyway, this is our first outing that's not work-related," he remarked, hoping to divert Joanne's attention back to their evening together. But he felt increasingly on edge. Every so often, he'd catch glances thrown his way from Mr. Jones' table, and even from others in the room. But one particular individual caught his eye and almost made him spit out his drink. The dashing man in a striking red tuxedo, seated behind Joanne, was also eyeing him intently. What were the odds that one of his fellow investors would be here tonight of all nights?

In the past, Xavier's friendly demeanor meant that when dining with friends, acquaintances would often stop by their table for a quick chat. But tonight, he hoped his more reserved posture would deter any unwanted interactions. If too many patrons struck up conversations with him, and Joanne overheard even snippets, she might piece together the whole picture.

Joanne's finger glided down the menu's length. "It is," she mused, her gaze lifting to meet his, eyes shimmering under the soft radiance of the chandelier. The makeup she wore tonight accentuated her features just right. The wing-tipped eyeliner, in particular, tugged at Xavier's heart. While he appreciated seeing her all dressed up, every iteration of Joanne held its own unique beauty to him. She paused, a slight smile playing on her lips, "I have to admit, it feels a bit surreal being out here with you."

The bearded man, whom Xavier recognized as one of his investors, flashed a knowing grin in his direction. Trying to play it cool, Xavier offered a subtle salute, which drew a puzzled look from Joanne. "Sorry, just an acquaintance. He's seated behind you, but you don't need to look—" However, even before he finished his sentence, Joanne had already turned to sneak a glance. Xavier sighed inwardly, scratching his head in mild exasperation.

Joanne faced forward again. "His suit looks amazing," she commented. At her back, Xavier's friend looked away, flooding Xavier's system with relief. It seemed Xavier's 'people magnet' was off tonight. "How are you friends with Peachwood's higher-ups *and* the everyday folk?" she asked, taking a piece of garlic bread from the basket in the middle of the table.

Taking a piece of garlic bread, Xavier savored a bite before responding. "I've always believed in connecting with people for who they are, not where they stand in societal ranks," he said, pulling out a handkerchief to lightly dab at his forehead. Once he'd replaced it in his pocket, he continued, "Regarding our out-of-work interaction," he began, leaning forward slightly, capturing her attention. "I don't find it odd at all. It's just us, out of our usual work attire, free from restrictions." His voice held a touch of warmth and charm, hoping to put her at ease and set the tone for the rest of their evening.

Joanne quirked an eyebrow, a hint of mischief in her eyes. "What were our restrictions before?"

"You know, the boundaries set by the professional setting, our roles at Roasted Beans," Xavier began, pausing for a moment to gather his thoughts. "Out here, away from the café, it's just you and me. Xavier, hopelessly smitten, and Joanne, gracious enough to share her evening with him."

To his surprise, a genuine laugh bubbled up from Joanne. It was a sound he hadn't heard from her before. "Was that a pity laugh, Ms. Richards?" he teased, raising his drink.

As he took a sip, his gaze naturally drifted across the room. Eddie and his table were engrossed in their meal, and his investor friend seemed deep in conversation, allowing Xavier to refocus on the captivating woman in front of him. *Wait, who is he with?* Xavier squinted, leaning slightly to get a better view. He recognized those faces. The owners of the grocery stores that dotted Main Street. This wasn't just a casual dinner; it bore the trappings of a business meeting. A realization clicked in Xavier's mind: expansion. And that spacious warehouse on Pete's Lane would probably serve as the perfect location for a new branch. But that speculation wasn't his concern. Well, unless they decided to pull him into the conversation, seeking his insights.

Wanting to avoid drawing any attention to himself, Xavier subtly shifted, using Joanne as a sort of shield from their view. The last thing he needed was to get roped into another business discussion on what was supposed to be a casual evening out.

Joanne's laughter subsided, and with a playful toss of her curly hair, she glanced over her shoulder towards the back table. "Is your friend trying to get your attention again?" she asked, a lingering chuckle tinting her words.

"No," Xavier said quickly, clapping his hands together to draw her gaze back to him. She looked slightly taken aback by the abruptness. "Apologies. Thought I saw a mosquito," he said, feigning annoyance while subtly wiping his hands on his tie.

Shifting the conversation back to her earlier reaction, he wore a sly grin. "Back to that laugh of yours," Xavier began, the playful twinkle in his eyes evident. "Am I funny now?"

Joanne waved off the idea with a playful swipe of her hands. "Hardly," she countered, though there was a hint of teasing in her tone. "The thought of you being completely smitten with me? It's just amusing," she remarked. Beneath the playful exterior, Xavier noticed a touch of shyness, a hint of vulnerability. Her attempt to keep a straight face failed as a hint of a smile threatened to emerge.

"And just how long have you been harboring this... interest?" she inquired, her eyes dancing with mischief. Just as Xavier was about to answer, the waiter appeared, ready to take their order, adding another layer of anticipation to the moment.

Handing his menu to the waiter, Xavier hesitated for a moment, collecting his thoughts. "Would it seem too forward if I admitted it was from the moment I met you?" He felt a flush of warmth spreading across his face, a sensation that was amplified by the look of genuine surprise on Joanne's face. And yet, her wide-eyed, almost incredulous expression was endearing in its own right.

"It does sound a bit sappy when said out loud," he admitted with a wry chuckle, attempting to keep his composure. Even though her presence had a way of softening his edges, he was determined to keep some semblance of cool. After all, it wouldn't do to let her know just how deeply she affected him.

"I'm actually flattered," Joanne played with her water, a hint of a smile forming. "So, all this time, I've been giving orders to a man smitten with me? Why didn't that put you off?" she asked, a touch of playful disbelief in her voice. "In my experience, most guys aren't too thrilled about being bossed around by their crush." Taking a sip, her eyebrows raised slightly in appreciation. "This water is good," she remarked, referencing the menu's note about its Fijian spring source.

Xavier met her gaze with unwavering confidence. "I'm not like most guys, Joanne. I'm Xavier. A man who finds strength and conviction attractive," he responded, recalling a past conversation. The idea that she might've seen him as dismissive or condescending weighed on him. He hoped tonight would dispel any such notions.

"Humph. You ignored all of my rules, so I guess that speaks for itself."

"You know why I did that Joanne, come on," Xavier chuckled, dabbing his mouth with the meticulously folded napkin. She behaved in a playfully stubborn manner that drove him insane. In the best way of course. "I have to ask, though: why did you agree to this dinner? Just tell me that, and I promise I won't press any further."

She took some time before answering. His heart fluttered as light bounced off her glossed lips. "You were easy to talk to and sweet with me when I needed it," she stared at the neighboring tables. "You also bared your darkest trials to me just to help me feel better. I liked that. You impressed me, so I decided why not?" She smiled, something he wished he'd see more of.

A stint of silence fell between them. They simply perceived each other as it lingered. Caring not for people's conversations or the mellow music permeating the background.

"Are you glad you said yes?" Xavier leaned forward, resting his arms on the table. The faint scent of his cologne wafted up, and he found himself wondering if she approved. Maybe he'd applied a bit much, but he wanted everything to be just right tonight. As he considered this, the soft fragrance she wore reached him, adding to the perfect ambiance he'd hoped for. He just wanted everything to be perfect.

"No, this is too weird," Joanne began, her voice even. Xavier's heart sank, the weight of disappointment pressing down on him. But then her eyes danced with mischief. "I'm joking," she admitted with a playful chuckle. "So far, it's been great. I'm looking forward to our meal and learning more about you."

The weight of realization bore down on him. Despite their months of interaction, Joanne had only glimpsed the tip of the iceberg that was Xavier. She was aware of some of his struggles, yes, but the vast depths of his life remained unknown. As the noise of Mr. Jones and his investor friend blended with the ambient hum, a pang of anxiety stirred within Xavier. How much of himself was he ready to unveil to Joanne? And more importantly, how would she react when faced with the entirety of who he was? The thought both excited and unnerved him.

Over the course of their meal, their conversations traversed the realms of schoolyard memories, past relationships, and cherished friendships. With every shared anecdote, Joanne seemed to let down her guard a touch more, revealing facets of herself that Xavier had never seen. It was akin to witnessing a delicate blossom gradually unfurling under the soft touch of dawn. In that intimate setting, amid the gentle hum of other diners and the distant clink of cutlery, Xavier felt a profound sense of gratitude. The atmosphere in the restaurant, with its soft lighting and muted conversations, seemed to cocoon them, drawing them into a world of their own.

As their dinner progressed, Xavier found himself leaning forward, entirely captivated by Joanne's stories about her friends.

"But why did she do that knowing you'd hate it?" He couldn't contain his laughter. The tales of Joanne's friends were a unique blend of chaos and comedy that was proving to be pure entertainment.

Joanne paused, playfully sipping from her spoon before answering, her eyes sparkling with mischief. "Because Nevaeh thrives on pushing my buttons. It's like her life's calling, even if she won't admit it," she shared, her voice dripping with a mix of exasperation and fondness. "But thank goodness for Brandi. She put Nevaeh in her place after that wild prank. Otherwise, I swear, I would've given Nevaeh a piece of my mind," she said, punctuating her statement with a faux slap in the air.

"You wouldn't do that. Be for real," Xavier teased, setting down his fork. Each bite of his Wagyu Beef had been a culinary journey, a decadent treat he was more than willing to splurge on. After all, he'd made it clear from the start that tonight was on him. Joanne was the kind of woman who deserved nothing short of the best, not just tonight, but every day.

"Believe me, I've had my moments," she said, motioning in the air with her hand. "Back when we were teens, I'd give her a little nudge or a tug on her ponytail when she teased too much. But I always tried to keep it light-hearted," Joanne's gaze dropped, focused intently on her soup. "I just wanted to make sure it remained play-ful. Actions and intentions matter, and I didn't want to be like my father," she mused, taking a thoughtful sip of her soup.

Xavier needed no explanation to understand what she meant. "You've got a good heart, Joanne. You'd never intentionally harm anyone. You believe that, don't you?" As he spoke, the distant sound of chairs scraping caught his ear, signaling the departure of the Sky High Real Estate team.

"I know," Joanne said, dabbing at her lips with her napkin, the intricate crane fold now a memory. "And what about you? Everyone in Peachwood adores you, but there must be someone who really tests your patience? I don't mean to say I can't stand Nevaeh, but you know what I'm getting at."

Mr. Jones and Eddie approached their table. "Big man Xavier. You should have joined us for dinner," said Mr. Jones in his top hat and tux.

Xavier hid his irritation. Eddie tapped Xavier's arm while cack-ling with Jones. Joanne seemed lost on why they interrupted. "Maybe next time. Tonight, I'm a bit preoccupied," he said, nodding towards Joanne with a gentle smile. She responded with a warm grin of her own. "You fellas take care now," Xavier added, as hee stood clasping Eddie's hand and giving him a friendly pat on the back. "Better hurry. Looks like your group's leaving you behind," he added, nodding toward their departing colleagues near the entrance.

Mr. Jones bowed slightly at Joanne. "Pleasure to meet you again, Ms. Richards. I've had your coffee, and it is *delightful*," he grabbed Xavier's shoulder. "You're lucky this guy approved of—"

Xavier interrupted with a loud cough, his gaze sharp. "Thank you for the kind words, gentlemen. But I think it's time for you to make your exit," he urged, sensing Joanne's inquisitive look.

Eddie, however, wouldn't be deterred. "Why rush us off, Xavier? At the very least, make a proper introduction to this captivating creature," he exclaimed, fluttering his fingers in Joanne's direction.

Her scowl deepened, and she dropped her spoon with a clatter. "Creature? I'm a person. Is that your idea of a compliment?" she shot back, her accusing gaze fixed on Xavier as if Eddie's words were somehow his responsibility.

Xavier felt a pang of frustration at his friend's choice of words. "Eddie, that was completely uncalled for. Apologize immediately. You can't go around calling people creatures," he reprimanded. In his peripheral vision, he caught his fellow investor rising. The man did a wave and strode to Xavier. His companions followed gladly. *Not now. Please.*

"Okay, okay. I'm sorry. It wasn't my intention to offend anyone," Eddie said, grabbing his chest for emphasis. "So, are you two together?" The invasive question worsened Xavier's falling mood.

Joanne's response was succinct and straightforward. "We're on a date," she stated plainly, her expression giving nothing away.

Xavier had reached his limit with the awkward situation and discreetly signaled the waiter to approach. As the waiter approached their table, Xavier made a swift decision. "Please pack up our food. We're leaving," he requested, his tone firm.

When the investor came closer, Xavier waved him off, not in the mood to entertain further conversation. Turning his attention back to Joanne, he abruptly changed the course of their evening. "Joanne, I have a better idea for our date. Do you like picnics?" he asked, ignoring the bewildered expressions of his friends and the surprise on Joanne's face. He was aware of how sudden this might seem, but he wasn't ready to reveal everything tonight, not when he felt they were finally connecting. The nervousness coursing through him was palpable, but he was determined to change the mood and create a memorable moment for Joanne.

As Joanne suddenly shot to her feet, the investor and his clients observed the scene in silence, still taken aback by the unexpected turn of events. Joanne's voice rose in protest, her frustration evident.

"What? You can't just change our date plan in the middle of it," she exclaimed, her bowl in hand. "We agreed to have dinner. And who says I want to leave? Where is this coming from?" Her voice softened as she continued, "I thought we were having fun," her initial anger slowly giving way to confusion and disappointment.

Lenny, the investor, intervened, his frown deepening. "Xavier, is everything all right with you?" He acknowledged Joanne with a nod. "I saw you and thought you might want to weigh in on this decision the Edwards are making," he added, stepping aside to reveal the affluent couple.

Xavier's throat tightened as Joanne absentmindedly rubbed her arms. "Lenny, I'm occupied at the moment. I'm sorry to say this, but now is just not the time," he replied, declining the request for assistance, a departure from his usual willingness to help. He noticed Lenny's surprised reaction but refrained from apologizing. The curious glances from onlookers were becoming more noticeable. If he didn't extricate himself from the situation soon, they might escort him out.

Turning his attention back to Joanne, he attempted to whisper an apology. "Joanne, I'm sorry this is so sudden, but I just want some privacy," he explained softly, although their company could still overhear his words.

Mr. Jones seemed to take the hint and grabbed Eddie's arm. "Nice seeing you, Xavier. You have a good evening," he said as he left hastily taking Eddie with him. The investor made his exit with the Edwards, promptly bidding Xavier farewell. Xavier was worried he had offended them, but he had more important things to stress about.

Joanne's unsaid words spoke volumes. She tapped her shoe in impatience, clearly in wait of some clarification.

Overwhelmed by the fear of revealing the truth, Xavier turned his gaze away. "I think you'd like where I live," he said, his voice heavy with a sigh. "I'm sorry for how abrupt this is. Would you consider relocating?" He let the soft melodies of the restaurant fill the ensuing silence. "I just felt uncomfortable being surrounded by friends on our date. I wanted tonight to be more intimate," he admitted, with most of what he said being true, though he left out crucial details.

Joanne appeared less perturbed by the sudden change of plans. "You know what?" She shrugged, offering a small smile that lifted Xavier's spirits. It was a relief to see that she didn't seem to hold any ill feelings toward him. "I get what you mean. I've felt like I'm on display all night," she added, her teasing tone lightening the mood. "It's almost like you're a celebrity," she quipped playfully.

"I really am not," he insisted, his nerves causing him to perspire more than usual. "Trust me, Joanne, Xavier Evans is just an ordinary man who happens to be well known," he replied, downplaying his own accomplishments with a modesty that hardly matched his true achievements.

CHAPTER SEVENTEEN

As they arrived at their destination, Xavier couldn't help but feel relieved. They had spent the car ride singing along to pop hits, and one of the highlights had been discovering their shared love for RnB pop music. Styrofoam bowls filled with dessert sat behind them. Xavier had made the decision to get dessert before heading to their moonlight picnic, ensuring they had treats to enjoy. He hoped that this romantic dessert date beneath the starry sky would help make up for the earlier awkwardness.

Joanne had been humming and tapping her fingers on the car door. She sang a stream of 'la's to herself before glancing out of the window. Xavier had parked outside his front gate, and the streets in this neighborhood were known for their tranquility. Some distant homes were visible across and beside the massive black gate, but they were far off. The gate itself resembled the entrance of a hotel, complete with a communication unit for speaking. Beyond it lay a vast estate with numerous houses. Xavier often stayed at his other home in Peachwood, but had chosen this one tonight for its spacious yard. They would need to drive to reach it, as Xavier's house was situated at the very back of the property.

Joanne's singing came to a dramatic halt. "Wait."

Xavier could guess. "I know the gate looks intimidating, but behind it is paradise," he put his neck out the window. "George, it's me. Can you open up? I have someone very special who's ready for a picnic," he said, winking at Joanne, whose mouth hung open. At this, the gears in his brain moved faster. This wasn't your everyday amazement, was it?

As George opened the front gate, Xavier drove his car into the estate. Garden lanterns illuminated the lush yards that lined the roads, and the driveways were paved with beige bricks of various shades. Xavier's car glided smoothly past the houses, but Joanne's expression had shifted to one of horror.

"Is everything okay?" he asked, concerned by her reaction.

Joanne opened her palms in a gesture of confusion. "I'm just trying to figure out if this really is the same estate I live in or if there's another estate that looks identical to it because on our drive here, I was wondering why the route felt familiar, and now here we are," she explained.

Xavier's blood ran cold as he had a sudden realization. "Oh, goodness," he breathed, his heart racing. He accelerated ahead, his mind racing even faster. The reason Joanne had found an affordable guest house was because of him. Xavier had advertised a newly constructed home on his estate specifically for Joanne. How could he forget that this was where she lived? He had gone to such lengths to avoid potential revelations at the restaurant, only to now realize his own foolishness.

"How long have you lived here?" Joanne questioned, her gaze penetrating. Xavier could sense that she had seen through him, and for a brief moment, he considered lying. But with everything that had transpired, Joanne had her suspicions. First, he abruptly left dinner, and now he lived in the same estate as her. The poor woman looked utterly bewildered.

"Is this some kind of prank?" Joanne continued, her voice tinged with disbelief. "You packed up our dessert just to bring me home early?" She was trying to make sense of the situation, and Xavier knew he needed to come clean.

Xavier's tongue felt as heavy as a ship anchor as he struggled to respond. "No. Of course not. I live here too. We're almost to my place. See?" he said, stepping on the gas pedal and accelerating toward his distant house. "I guess we've been neighbors but never realized?" he added, his voice wavering as he told a blatant lie. He wished he could be honest with her, but fear held him back.

Joanne's lips tightened into a thin line, and every trace of joy vanished from her perfect face. Xavier had worked with her long enough to recognize when he had upset her.

"Xavier, what on earth is going on?" she demanded, her frustration evident.

Xavier lifted his foot off the accelerator and squeezed the steering wheel tightly. His hands grew numb, but he didn't care. His heart raced, and finally, he decided to come clean.

"I'll explain when we get to the house. Just hold on," he said, his voice filled with unease and uncertainty.

Finally, they arrived at Xavier's home. Without wasting any time, he led Joanne to the backyard. He spread a thick blanket on the grass and motioned for her to join him. Xavier took a seat and set down their treats. Above them, clusters of stars spread out for miles, their brightness almost otherworldly. The stars cast a gentle light onto the well-maintained yard, with his basket-shaped hedges meticulously trimmed. Xavier and Joanne sat side by side, with the back porch behind them. A gentle breeze wafted through the sliding doors, neither cold nor warm, but just a tender puff of air. The unusual weather seemed to complement their picnic, though Xavier couldn't help but feel a sense of unease as he prepared to confess everything to Joanne.

"Okay, you've got me sitting all cozy in this amazing yard under the starlit sky. Is this all a ploy to soften the blow?" Joanne's angry words heightened Xavier's stress levels. "Is what you're going to say bad? What is all this, and why did we really leave the restaurant?"

she continued, moving uncomfortably close and mirroring his anxiety with a veil of anger concealing her own.

Understanding her fears and concerns given her personality, Xavier reached out and took Joanne's hand. "Trust me. It's not anything horrifying I'm about to tell you," he assured her, feeling the need to explain quickly, like ripping off a band-aid. Keeping her in suspense would only hurt her. "I just haven't been completely honest with you," he added, stretching his feet, concealed in expensive leather shoes, forward.

Joanne fell silent, waiting for him to continue.

"Joanne..." Xavier finally mustered the courage to reveal his big secret. "The truth is that nothing that's happened here has been a coincidence. I'm a real estate investor, and the post office you bought for Roasted Beans was previously owned by me. The men back at the restaurant were trying to say that I'd approved the sale. This entire estate is mine, too. I put the house you currently stay in up for sale after I discovered you wanted a place here in Peachwood. I deliberately got a job at your coffee shop because I wanted to help you. I wanted to make sure that our dear post office got replaced by something just as special."

With that confession, the cat was out of the bag, and the only sound that filled the night was the deafening chirping of crickets hidden in the grass.

Xavier, for the life of him, couldn't read her reaction. "Will you say something soon?" Tonight may have been warm, but his body felt icy. Their first date shouldn't have been the moment he revealed everything. For so long, he'd wanted intimate time with Joanne, yearning for a chance to be alone with her outside of work. Why did it have to go so wrong? They'd had fun over dinner, but he felt like he might die if tonight ended up being their last night out. He could sense her disdain for liars, and he feared the worst. Why hadn't he shared this information earlier? They had been opening up to each other, and she might not have despised him if he had been honest from the start.

His heart pounded inside his chest, making him feel sick. "Joanne, I—" he began, his voice trembling with anxiety.

"Wow," Joanne laughed sardonically. "So, this whole time you've been lying to me?" She cut him off as he tried to explain. "That's why those rich people knew you back there. They knew you as a big-shot investor. Ugh!" She face-palmed, dragging her palm from her forehead to the tip of her chin. "And you thought that I'd be helpless at running a business worthy of replacing your precious post office because I'm not a successful investor like you. Is that it? Is that the truth behind all of your efforts at 'helping?'" She made air quotes with her fingers, her frustration and disappointment evident in her voice.

Now we're back to square one, Xavier thought, feeling the weight of his own words as they reversed all the progress they had made during their date. He knew he had to clarify his intentions.

"No, Joanne, I meant nothing ill by it. It was never my intention to hurt you. And like I keep saying, I believe in your capabilities. There's never been a doubt in my mind that you were a gifted businesswoman," he said earnestly, gripping her hand tighter. "Please, I didn't want to tell you because—"

"You thought I'd only care about what's in your pockets?" She removed her hand from his, her disappointment palpable in her voice.

Xavier's voice wavered as he desperately tried to explain himself. "Of course not!" He felt the weight of his mistakes pressing down on him. "I didn't want to tell you because I was sure you'd be less receptive of me if you knew that I owned the property," he confessed, running a hand through his disheveled hair. "Granted, you'd been unreceptive regardless, but I was certain you'd never hire an investor. Joanne, I just really wanted to help. This has nothing to do with seeing you as incapable. We've been over this. I know what Peachwood Grovers like, so it only made sense."

He attempted a smile, but it wobbled under the circumstances. This couldn't be the end for them. Xavier was determined to fight for their connection, but he also understood that he couldn't be too pushy. If Joanne truly despised him for his lies, he'd have to respect her decision and let go.

Joanne's face contorted with pain as she shot a glare at Xavier, her eyes filled with conflict. For what felt like an eternity, silence hung in the air. Finally, she looked away and let out a deep sigh. "I don't know," she admitted, her voice trembling with uncertainty.

Xavier moved closer, his heart pounding with hope. "What don't you know?" he pressed gently. "Please, tell me. We can talk through this." He was willing to do anything to salvage their connection, to hold onto something beautiful that felt like it was slipping through his fingers. He couldn't bear the thought of letting her go.

Xavier felt like he was walking on a tightrope, teetering between despair and hope as he listened to Joanne's conflicted words. Her eyes, dark and searching, examined the blanket as if it held the answers to the questions swirling in her mind.

"Lying is awful," she began, her voice heavy with the weight of her emotions. "Knowing that you fooled me for so long is driving me crazy, but at the same time..." Her hand clenched into a fist on the red checkered cloth, and she pounded it once before letting it fall limply.

"I can tell better than anyone that your intentions were pure," she continued, her gaze finally meeting Xavier's. But there was a spark of distrust in her eyes, a wariness that pierced through the moment. Her eyes trembled and squinted, like those of a stray animal that had been abandoned one time too many.

"Isn't that all that matters?" Xavier asked, his voice filled with a sense of longing as he looked out into the peaceful night. It felt like they were the only two people in the world at that moment, and he hoped to make amends for his mistakes.

"Look, I'm really sorry about what I did," he continued, his words sincere and heartfelt. "You have every right to be mad, but if you give me a second chance, I'll never ever lie to you again. I'll be completely and utterly honest moving forward."

He gently reached out and undid her clenched fist with his fingers, his hand coming to rest against hers. "Please reopen your heart to let me in?" he implored, his touch warm against her cooling skin.

Joanne didn't pull her hand away. Instead, she accepted his tender gesture, her fingers intertwining with his. "Okay, fine," she responded, feigning reluctance as she averted her gaze. But there was a small, playful smile playing on her lips, a secret she couldn't hide. Xavier couldn't help but admire how her lips glistened under the starlight.

"But it's only because I'm curious to see how we'll work," she continued, inching closer to him on the blanket. "And because you've been a big help with the shop," her words were soft, almost lost in the quietness of the night.

Xavier's heart swelled with joy, and he playfully nudged Joanne's shoulder. "What was that last part?" he teased, leaning in closer as if to catch her whispered words.

Joanne tapped his arm lightly, her laughter joining his. "Don't get a big head about it," she said, her eyes sparkling with warmth and humor.

Xavier's muscles relaxed as he appreciated her understanding. He reclined further, his hands supporting his upper body. "We have these desserts packed up. Would you like to start eating them, or has the time passed?" he inquired, gazing up at the starry night sky.

Joanne reached for the dessert containers. "We'd be fools not to chow down. Here," she handed Xavier his dessert. "The hard part is over," she added, popping open her bowl. She sniffed its contents and continued, "Unless there's some other secret you'd like to share with me," she narrowed her eyes, a hint of playfulness in her tone. "Whatever else you're hiding, you need to say now. I don't want any other surprises," she said as she stuck her fork into her strawberry shortcake.

Xavier savored his chocolate dessert, impressed by its perfect temperature. He couldn't help but wink at her. "Trust me. There's nothing else to confess," he assured her. "What I revealed just now wasn't as bad as some secrets I've had to listen to," he shuddered slightly, reminiscing.

"Eh?" Joanne responded with a mouthful of frosting. "What do you mean?" she asked, her curiosity piqued.

Xavier continued sharing stories about his past, particularly one about a girl he had met in university who had been less than truthful about her hobbies and her life. He went into great detail, even describing the girl's ex-boyfriend who had been part of the story. Joanne listened attentively, reacting at appropriate moments and laughing at his humorous anecdotes.

After Xavier's tale, Joanne reciprocated by sharing her own story about a high school boyfriend named Wes, who had been a serial liar. Xavier felt a pang of empathy for her, knowing she had been deceived, but it was clear that she had moved past the experience. In their current moment, they could laugh together at the absurdity of the people who had wronged them, a much-needed exchange after their earlier argument.

As they continued their conversation, it felt like they were old friends catching up on past experiences. Xavier couldn't help but feel reassured by Joanne's openness. It was evident that she trusted him, and despite the small hiccup they had experienced earlier, their connection remained strong.

Joanne couldn't contain her laughter as Xavier shared the story of his rebellious phase in high school. She covered her face with her empty bowl, her heels neatly placed on the grass as she sat with her knees bent on the ground.

Xavier, feeling completely at ease, had removed his shoes and sat with his legs crossed. He reminisced, "He grounded me, of course. I was completely out of line. I can't believe I tried to sneak out." He relished in Joanne's bouts of laughter, finding her joy infectious. "I got what I deserved when he pulled up at the house party. I don't think a cheetah competing in the Olympics could have caught up to me with how fast I ran out of there."

Joanne, still chuckling, playfully asked, "I bet he chased after you, right?"

Xavier nodded vigorously, confirming her assumption, which led to more laughter from both of them. As Joanne's laughter subsided, Xavier couldn't help but be captivated by her. From head to toe, she was a work of art, and she had him completely entranced.

"I almost cried on that one," she said as she dried her wet eyes. "I think you'd get along with my friends. They're all completely insane like you." She gently fist-bumped his shoulder. "Or at least teenage you would have gotten along with them."

Xavier stretched out on the blanket, lying on his back with his arms behind his head. He gazed up at the clusters of stars forming shapes above them. He imagined a world similar to this one, where a version of himself stared back, pondering the existence of life beyond. The universe was indeed incredible. He grinned at Joanne and playfully waved at her. "Come on. Lie next to me."

"In this dress?" Joanne pinched the stretchy material of her dress.

Xavier grinned playfully. "You can lie back in that dress. In fact, it's perfect for it. It'll keep your legs in place," he said, wanting to show her something special.

After some contemplation, Joanne stretched out beside him, her head next to his. He couldn't help but feel a rush of butterflies in his belly. "Wow. The stars are even prettier when you look at them like this," she said in awe.

"That's what I wanted to show you," he said, raising a finger. "I'm no expert, but I do like making shapes. Look at my fingers while they connect the dots. Try to guess what I'm making, okay?"

Joanne teased, "Oh, so we're preschoolers now?"

Xavier couldn't resist a playful jab. "What? No, we're not. Hey," he said, noticing her mischievous smile, "just because we're adults doesn't mean we can't have fun or play games. Don't restrict your-self so much."

"I don't need a lecture from you," Joanne retorted, pointing at something. "I'll play along. I was only teasing. Let me go first so you see how it's done," she said, closing one eye.

Xavier chuckled, truly enjoying Joanne's sense of humor. "You act like you've played this game when I literally just made it up," he said, crossing his arms.

"It's just connect-the-dots with stars," Joanne began tracing. "Look closely."

Xavier followed her every move and tried to discern the stars she connected. "Okay, judging by how you moved, I'm just going to say that you drew an ice cream cone."

Joanne sat up, amused. "Ice cream cone?" Her tone implied disbelief. "How did you get that?" She snorted. "It's a snowman."

Xavier joined her in sitting up. "Oh," he admitted, scratching his arm. "Psh. Joanne, those two things have the same shape."

"No, they don't. Snowmen don't have triangles attached. What, can you not draw?"

Her comment caught him off guard, and he couldn't help but burst into laughter. Xavier lowered his face, trying to hide his amusement. "Joanne, how are you like this even in games?" he asked, finally composing himself and wiping away tears of laughter.

Joanne's laughter was stifled, and she shrugged. "If you don't like whatever 'this' is, then you can—" Her words were interrupted when Xavier shushed her with a finger and leaned closer.

Unintentionally sporting a devilish smirk, Xavier closed in on his date, maintaining eye contact. "Don't get it twisted," he whispered softly. "I love it."

Joanne fell silent for a moment, her lips tantalizingly close. She narrowed the tiny gap between them. "You love what exactly?" she asked, her voice just above a whisper.

Xavier was intoxicated by their proximity. He wanted to hold her but didn't want to overstep her boundaries. He waited, allowing her to take the lead. "I love..." His lips were almost brushing against hers. Her inviting, lush lips were so close, tempting him. He dared not make the first move, wanting her to guide this moment.

Submissiveness wasn't his usual style, but for her, he was willing to be whatever she wanted. He inspected her pupils and her sultry expression, wondering what was going through her mind. "I love when you tease me. When you tell me off," he confessed, his voice filled with sincerity. "It sounds strange, but I appreciate every side of Joanne."

Joanne's attention was suddenly drawn to something in the sky. "Xavier, look!" she gasped, her eyes wide with excitement. She sat up and tucked a strand of hair behind her ear. "I've never seen one in person," she exclaimed. "Look before it disappears. I thought they were made up at some point, but look at that!" Her unbridled joy mirrored that of a child experiencing their first taste of ice cream or riding a roller coaster.

"I'm looking, I'm looking," Xavier replied, torn between watching the shooting star and admiring the beautiful sight of Joanne. What were the odds of a shooting star gracing their picnic? He wanted to watch it with her, as he had difficulty tearing his gaze away from her. Her newfound sense of freedom and joy was a captivating sight. He had never seen her so carefree and full of life, and it warmed his heart.

"Make a wish," he softly encouraged her as the ball of gleaming light gradually faded. He didn't want Joanne's inner child to miss this precious moment. Although he believed in keeping wishes as personal secrets, Xavier couldn't help but wonder what she had wished for. Silently, he prayed that whatever it was, it would come true.

When Joanne opened her eyes gently, a warm and fuzzy sensation filled Xavier's heart. She looked at him with a certain glow about her, and he found himself lost in her gaze. He longed for her to say something, to break the silence and let him know what was on her mind. The moment felt magical, and he didn't want it to end.

Her eyelids fell, and she bent towards him, giving Xavier what he needed. At last, he gave in to temptation and touched her lower chin. Doing so spurred her to close both eyes. He unintentionally shut his, too. Leaning in, Xavier tilted his head and connected his lips to hers.

In his mind, he'd envisioned a simple smooch. About three seconds would do it. He'd just wanted to taste her and for her to taste him. But the second they kissed, fireworks exploded. The moment their lips met, Xavier was lost in the intoxication of her kiss. Her lips were so soft, so warm against his own. He reached up to cradle her face in his hands as the kiss deepened, both of them melting into each other. Joanne's arm encircled his neck, pulling him closer as their mouths moved together hungrily. Xavier's pulse raced and heat coursed through his veins at her touch. He was drowning in her, forgetting everything else around them. Joanne's fingers threaded through his hair, eliciting a soft groan from him. Their kisses grew more urgent, more passionate as weeks of longing finally overflowed. Xavier trailed his lips along the curve of her jaw as she sighed his name. Lowering to the mat, they came together in a tangle of lips, limbs, and racing hearts.

They'd gone way over Xavier's planned three seconds. When they finally broke apart, both were panting and disheveled. Her hair stuck out wildly from where his hands had threaded through it. His tie hung loose around his undone collar as he tried to catch his breath. Lying on their sides, the world narrowed to just the two of them. Xavier stared, transfixed by the sheen of sweat on her lip, the rapid rise and fall of her chest. The cooling night air chilled the sweat trickling down his own back. He didn't want this moment to end.

"Your place isn't too far," he finally managed between labored breaths. "Want me to drive you?"

Joanne's eyes fluttered closed once more. "If you have room, I won't mind staying over."

Xavier's heart leaped. Unable to contain his smile, he nodded eagerly. "Then be my guest."

He leaned in to capture her lips once more, already addicted to her intoxicating kisses. This was a beginning he never wanted to end.

CHAPTER EIGHTEEN

Golden morning light filtered in through the expansive glass doors, tickling Joanne awake. Beyond the panes, vibrant gardens bloomed, flowers in full riotous colors reaching for the sun. Birds twittered and took to the skies, soaring over the manicured lawns of Xavier's neighborhood.

Joanne shifted under the cool, silky sheets, suddenly aware of herself. She sat up, clutching the scarlet bedding to her chest as memories of last night flooded back. Xavier's bedroom felt sterile, impersonal—beige carpets ending abruptly at the doorway, the bare dresser likely empty, his cavernous closet holding no personal effects. This wasn't a home, merely one of his many properties.

Her eyes traced over Xavier's sleeping form. His muscular arms were exposed above the sheets, his chiseled chest rising and falling with deep peaceful breaths. Conflicting emotions churned within Joanne as she watched him. She should feel anger at his months of deception, yet being here with him just felt right. His tender passion last night had set her body and heart ablaze, connecting them in ways she'd never experienced before.

Joanne sighed heavily, touching her lips as she recalled his warm kisses. She knew this was inappropriate - she was his boss, he'd lied about his wealth and life - but she couldn't deny her longing. Was she a fool to trust again so easily? To fall prey to his charm and abandon all caution? Joanne's doubts warred with her desire. She was scared of giving someone else such power over her again. Yet being near Xavier made her feel alive, made her want to give him anything he asked.

As his eyes slowly fluttered open, Joanne looked away, holding the sheets protectively higher. "Hey, morning," he rasped. Her heart-beat quickened at the sound of his sleep-roughened voice. In that moment, all her doubts vanished. She wanted nothing more than to lose herself in his arms again. To listen to him recount childhood stories or debate egg recipes over lazy weekend breakfasts. She was ready to take the leap, consequences be damned. "Morning," she whispered back shyly.

Xavier's signature mischief twinkled in his eyes and curved his lips. He sat up against the headboard, bare chest on display. Joanne longed to press her ear to it just to hear his heartbeat, to be close again. "I got the feeling you were an early riser," he said, touching the black satin durag atop his head. "Did you sleep well?"

Joanne smiled in spite of herself. Last night had been crazy yet exhilarating. "We had two dates in one and I made my first shooting star wish," something she never would have thought to do if not for him. Like a child, part of her had believed for a fleeting moment the wish might come true.

"It really was two dates in one - dinner, picnic," Xavier's scent washed over her, his cologne lingering on her own skin from their embrace. Fruity and icy mingled from their blended scents. "Does that mean we can't go out to the park today?" He pouted playfully. "I want to know if I've exceeded my date limit."

"Date limit," Joanne laughed, shaking her head. His charm and confidence made anger impossible. He'd been there when she was vulnerable, a steadfast comfort. Her instincts said he was no villain. She had to enjoy this, not let old trust issues sabotage something promising. His vow last night should have been enough - he'd never hurt her again. "And how am I supposed to dress for this second date? I don't suppose you have anything my size in those closets of yours." She nodded towards the bare white structure. "If there's anything at all in there."

Xavier stretched with a grunt before peeling back the sheets. "I keep a few outfits in every place of mine. I think my college jerseys might be in there." His boxers hugged his hips as he strode to the closet. "You'd look cute in one."

Joanne clutched the sheet to her chest, watching him skeptically. "You know full well I can't wear a man's shirt out." She feigned annoyance as he grabbed a massive blue one.

"Looks cozy, right?" Grinning, he brought it to the bed. "You can wear this for the drive home. I'll make breakfast then we can walk in the park if you want." Suddenly bashful, he scratched his arm without meeting her gaze. Mr. Confident couldn't make eye contact.

His sudden shyness endeared him to her. Joanne grabbed the oversized jersey and brought it to her nose, inhaling its scent. "Smells good for something that's been locked in a closet so long," she mused. The fabric engulfed her petite frame as she pulled it on and climbed from the bed. The hem hung past her hips, the sleeves swallowing her hands entirely.

She heard Xavier snort, his shoulders shaking with suppressed laughter. "What?" Joanne demanded, catching his amused expression. "What? Do I look stupid?" She hurriedly rolled up the sleeves to her elbows. "If I do, I'm not letting you drive me home in this thing." She scanned the room futilely for her own outfit from last night, lost in their passionate throes.

"No, you look adorable," Xavier assured her, taking her hands and appraising her bedhead fondly. "Even with your hair all messy like that." He leaned in swiftly to plant a kiss on her tousled locks before jogging towards the adjoining bathroom. "Follow me. You can get cleaned up in here."

Joanne felt herself blushing, suddenly self-conscious standing there swimming in his old college jersey. But the delight in his eyes at seeing her wear it was infectious. She couldn't help but grin and shake her head wryly at their silly domestic tableau - the oversized shirt, his teasing glances, sharing his bathroom to get ready. It all felt so natural, so right. As if waking up together like this could become a habit. A wonderfully tempting possibility.

THEIR FRIDAY NIGHT dinner had turned into a delightful weekend-long date. After their visit to the park, Joanne ended up staying over at Xavier's house on Saturday night. Xavier took it upon himself to give her a comprehensive tour of Peachwood, even though she had been living there for a few months. They explored various places, from cinemas to local eateries, and wherever they went, people seemed genuinely happy for Xavier. Joanne couldn't help but notice the whispers and smiles exchanged between onlookers. She would have felt self-conscious if it weren't for Xavier's wonderful company. Throughout their tour, he engaged her in meaningful conversations, mixing sweet words with intellectual discussions.

As their rendezvous extended into Sunday, Joanne felt like she was getting to know Xavier on a deeper, more spiritual level. They shared their thoughts, opinions, and engaged in lighthearted debates, never running out of topics to discuss. Conversations flowed naturally, and their connection grew stronger. When their Sunday adventure concluded, they returned to Xavier's house for a cozy movie night. They picked their favorite films at an old-school DVD rental store and prepared a delicious meal together.

As midnight approached, Joanne reluctantly packed her things to leave. Before parting ways, they exchanged a small, affectionate peck, promising to meet again during the week for another exciting date.

And indeed, they did.

December was swiftly passing by, evident in the changing

weather. The cool fall breeze had transformed into frigid winds, hinting at the imminent arrival of snow. Thick sweaters had replaced long fall jackets, and everyone ventured outside with their heads securely covered.

Joanne's arm was linked with Xavier's as they left work at sunset for an evening stroll around the block. The farmers and vendors were in the process of packing up their stands, having just passed the bustling farmer's market.

"It's looking promising, I must say," Joanne remarked, her gaze fixed on the horizon. "I didn't think it was possible, but I believe we'll actually meet our end-of-December goals." She couldn't help but smile, realizing that her once insufferable manager had turned out to be quite lovely. Dating Xavier had made her aware of the fact that she had made no friends in Peachwood. However, her days had brightened considerably with him by her side. At work, they still had their occasional arguments about running Roasted Beans, but it was all in good faith. Xavier's initiative had saved her business, so Joanne was making an effort to be more open-minded. This shift in mindset was new for her, but she was determined to adapt.

I used the word dating, but we haven't confirmed anything, Joanne thought as she stepped aside to let someone pass by; they weren't alone on the busy sidewalk. A lot of nine-to-fives had just ended, and employees were eager to get home. "Thank you for all of your help, Xavier," Joanne briefly rested her head on his arm.

He kissed her forehead with a smile, unashamedly displaying his affection. She hadn't realized she needed this from someone until Xavier. They had to be in a serious relationship. The intimacy and constant dates were a dead giveaway. A label was not required. "It's no problem. But don't give me all the credit. Remember who the genius businesswoman is," he greeted someone passing by. They turned a corner, their arms gradually unlocking. Xavier had mentioned taking her to Peachwood's frozen yogurt store. They had been there already, but he had noticed that Joanne liked it. She hadn't outwardly said so, but he was aware. She loved that about him too.

Joanne gladly accepted his compliment. "Of course. I haven't forgotten my worth, you know," she said, chin held high. "Just because I'm nicer doesn't mean I've forgotten my worth," she poked his strong arm. His at-home gym hadn't surprised her when she stayed at his place. Xavier was a man who valued a great physique.

"I know that for sure. How could you when you're worth more than a million?" he teased, though perhaps he was serious. When Xavier gave compliments, he went all in. And when he did, he always seemed serious. She liked that. Receiving praise daily boosted her self-esteem. She wasn't one to need a confidence boost, but she welcomed it anyway.

"Oh, stop it," Joanne giggled. They walked in silence for a moment, admiring the holiday decorations. An animatronic Santa waved on their way past a convenience store. Streamers and wreaths adorned certain buildings. She could already feel the joy of the season.

"So, what do you want for Christmas?" Xavier slipped his hand back into hers.

Joanne listened to the sound of their clicking footsteps and gazed at the overcast sky. "I'm usually more of a giver during the holidays."

"Really?"

"Yes. For me, I just enjoy buying gifts and seeing people react to them," memories of past Christmases replayed in her mind. She saw her friends smiling after opening her presents from her. "You see, I consider myself quite the gift-buying expert, and it's been proven that I am," butterflies fluttered wildly in her stomach. "Look out for the perfect gift from me this year, Xavier. I'll be getting you some-thing you never knew you wanted," she hid her rising excitement. Gift-shopping for loved ones was her way of showing appreciation. Adding Xavier to the list so soon made her blush. She wasn't one to rush into things, but he just had something special. And whatever it was, it completed her.

The man gasped. "Okay, someone's pretty confident. I'm getting goosebumps in anticipation," and that reaction was enough to pump her up. She couldn't wait to surprise him. "But you still haven't answered my question. There's got to be something you want," they were just a few feet from the yogurt store.

Joanne hummed in thought when they slowed down in front of it. Its glass doors opened, and teenagers skipped out, carrying short blue cups of strawberry yogurt. Their toppings excited Joanne. She loved gummy bears. "You don't have to get me anything. Don't hassle yourself," she tugged him inside.

Struck by the shop's warmth, they sighed with relief. Its lights clashed with the white tiled floors. The carol "Oh Christmas Tree" played softly in the background.

Xavier led them to the line, humming. He pinched the stubble on his chin. "You're not one to be upfront, so I'm going to take your non-answer to mean you want me to get you something incredible all on my own," he said smartly. "Am I right?"

Joanne pinched his arm. "I was serious about not wanting anything," she checked the menu. The last time they'd gotten blueberry yogurts with Skittles as a topping. This time she'd order something else. Xavier always let her order on his behalf. He trusted her in that regard. He'd said so himself.

"Oh, please," Xavier swatted the air in dismissal. "I'm sure that your friends get you gifts at Christmas. Don't you appreciate when they do? And be honest. If you got Ne—"

"I've said before that her full name is Nevaeh. You don't get to call her Nev because you're not her bestie," it cracked her up hearing him refer to Nevaeh by her nickname. He'd been confused about what to call her since the football match. She loved the ongoing joke but still wished he'd correct his mistake.

Xavier held his face, wincing. "Sorry. I meant Nevaeh. Nev just has a better ring to it," their interaction was but one in a sea of conversations. The teenagers seated along the walls were much louder than she and Xavier. Something about frozen yogurt made people happy. "I was saying that if you got Nev a gift and she didn't give one back, wouldn't you feel a sense of emptiness?"

Joanne stalled in answering. She saw his fake irritation and laughed. "No, honestly. For me, the gift of giving is gift enough," she crossed her arms, deciding on raspberry. She'd never had raspberry yogurt before. The forest cake flavor was tempting though. If only they could get them all.

He snorted when they went up one space. Four people stood ahead in the line. "So, you're just an angel then?" his warm hand took hers again. She turned to mush as his fingers massaged her knuckles. He did that a lot. Joanne could not express just how much she adored it. "You never want anything from anyone? I can't accept a gift from you and not give you one back."

"Well, get me something, Xavier," she said. "Even if it's a tacky vase, I'd love it. Because when it comes to other people, the thought is what counts," she grabbed her chest for emphasis. "But when it comes to me," Joanne's pitch dropped. "Getting the perfect present is all that matters. I know my friends and family. Every Christmas has to be perfect. Because I'm—"

"Perfect?" Xavier squished her hand. She felt small in his hold. His warm, soft hold. He hadn't removed his gloves. With how drastically the temperature had dropped, gloves were often worn outside. Joanne herself wore a pair too. She'd put them away after coming inside. "You're truly a magnificent woman and incredible person, but don't pressure yourself trying to achieve perfection," there he went with that voice of reason act. Only, it wasn't much of an act. During the weeks they'd grown closer, he'd become that for her. Someone who gave guidance and kept her in check. It wasn't in a condescending way at all. He'd be caring when grounding her in reality. "But I'm sure you understand better than anyone your talent for gift buying," he winked.

Joanne felt flushed. She fanned her neck then faced the person in front of her. "Are you okay having Raspberry yogurt this evening?"

"Is that what you want?"

She should have seen this coming. Her heart flipped when the question hit her ear. He'd put his lips there to ask. "Yes, Xavier. Why else would I ask you?" she looked up at him with an eyeroll.

He smiled. "Then yes. I'm completely okay with having raspberry."

Joanne considered the forest cake again. "You know what? Should we get the forest cake flavor instead? I want to try it but gummy bears taste better with fruit-based flavors," she wanted Xavier's opinion. Yes. Joanne had come very far.

Xavier held her shoulders. His thumbs naturally caressed them. "Which do you want more, my lady?"

She bit her bottom lip. The menu previews weren't helping. Both seemed mouth-watering. "I don't know. That's the thing. That's why I want your help. You can't just throw this back at me, Xavier," they went up in line again. Time was running out. "Help me out before I make the wrong choice," she shook her hands anxiously. Deciding what she wanted always came easily. Xavier's gift talk distracted her. *Don't blame him, Joanne. Don't blame him.*

"Here's the perfect solution," Xavier pointed from the forest cake picture to the raspberry. "You get the raspberry, and I get the forest cake. We take turns eating from each other's spoons," he rubbed down her arms. "Do you like that idea? It's all based on what you want."

Joanne tapped her forehead in chastisement. "Ugh! Why didn't I think of that?" It was so obvious. "I guess I overcomplicated what to get this time," she giggled while Xavier stared lovingly. His gaze sent pleasurable shudders down her back. "Thank you, Xavier."

"No problem. I'm always here for you."

CHAPTER NINETEEN

izza wasn't a particularly favored meal among their group, but that Saturday afternoon, Joanne and her friends had a strange craving for it. It might have been the climb in temperature with spring around the corner. After a drawn-out winter, its presence was welcome. The friends especially could not wait for summer.

Cheese on Nevaeh's slice clung to the piece she bit off. She stretched it high, to emphasize what happened. They shared a laugh at the spectacle. Luckily, they had the restaurant to themselves today. "Baked to perfection," Nevaeh gave the chef a thumbs up. He'd just finished wiping the front counter. They cheered on the bashful man who left for the kitchen. "Anyway, I'm just excited for what he'll surprise me with. I've had my eye on a brand-new pair of boots, but it was my intention to get them myself. Should I still buy them or wait to see his surprise in case he did?" she put down her half-eaten slice. Apart from the central pizza box, they'd asked for plates to rest their food. Each woman had a drink to sip from.

"Wait. It's obvious that that's the surprise, Nevaeh," Joanne shook the ice in her plastic cup of soda. "You've been having a hard time at work, and Sean noticed. He's doing his normal sweet fiancé thing by cheering you up with gifts," she'd believed that that went without saying. Through the single door to come into, they'd witness people stalking past on quick legs. Saturdays weren't restful days to Sweetgumers. Grocery shopping and special events took place on that day. This afternoon, a small talent show was scheduled to take place in town square. The fun never ended.

Nevaeh pursed her lips and shimmied her shoulders but agreed. Courtney and Brandi giggled at her reaction. "You didn't have to say it so roughly, but fine," her attitude immediately melted. "Ah! I'm getting new shoes. Sean is amazing! I think between him and Justin, he's the better fiancé," she stuck her tongue out at an offended Courtney.

"How so?" Courtney folded her pizza. She aimed it at Nevaeh with a frown. "Just because he gets you gifts? Justin gets gifts for me, too, Nev. Don't be out of line," she munched on her food. They'd ordered half extra cheese and half veggie today. "Let's not forget whose diamond is bigger," she sang.

"Ooo," Joanne jeered as Nevaeh's mouth dropped open in shock. She shot a smug glance at the equally stunned Brandi before cackling loudly. "Nevaeh, you asked for that one. Making it a competition like you always do." She snapped her fingers at Brandi. "See? I'm not the problem in our feud. Nevaeh has it out for everyone. She even got mild-mannered Courtney to snap."

They all laughed, and Nevaeh retaliated by pelting Joanne's face with napkins. Joanne fired back with whatever loose items she could grab from the table. "You want to start with me?" She set her drink down and threw her arms open wide.

"I'm ready!" Nevaeh jumped up comically, puffing out her chest.

Brandi shushed her as Courtney barked out a tense laugh, eyeing the front counter warily. "Just because we're the only ones here doesn't mean you can act like animals. Sit down, Nevaeh. Come on now." She snapped her fingers until Nevaeh plopped back down, snorting with residual giggles.

"Speaking of the fiancé-offs, when are you two actually getting married?" Brandi asked. "We've been helping you plan but haven't heard any dates." She batted her eyelashes at Courtney. "What's the holdup? Who's going first? I'm guessing whoever got proposed to first?"

Courtney scratched her head, intricate gold-threaded braids catching the light. "We're still happily engaged, guys. And crazy busy with the shop and art and...everything. But we'll get there and you'll all be invited, I promise."

Joanne took a sloppy bite of pizza

. "At this rate, I might get married before either of you," she remarked casually before sipping her drink.

Her friends paused, then slowly broke into excited smiles and chatter. "Where is this coming from? Is Xavier dropping hints?" Nevaeh asked eagerly. "It's been like seven months, right? I wouldn't be surprised if he pops the question soon."

Brandi pinched her chin thoughtfully as Joanne shook her head with a coy smile. "You two have been pretty inseparable though..."

"That was back when I had to constantly oversee the new shop," Joanne explained after taking a blissful bite of gooey pizza. She dabbed her mouth with a napkin before continuing. "Now that I'm only there twice a week, we don't go out as much." She licked her lips, tasting cherry gloss. "But we talk all the time. I just try not to distract him when I'm around the shop." Butterflies stirred, picturing Xavier's smile. Her friends grinned like children eyeing puppies, eager for details.

Joanne squirmed under their gazes. "I mean, we've been dating and texting, but..." She tugged at her shirt awkwardly. "To this day, we haven't exactly labeled ourselves a couple. I guess because a lot of our interactions involve the shop, but I don't know..." She forced a tight smile at Courtney. "I feel like I might be more interested than he is."

Dramatic gasps all around, Brandi covering her mouth in disbelief. "Joanne, how could you say that? He liked you first! He basically admitted to growing the business because he fell for you at first sight. Remember?" She swirled her straw through the fizzy liquid. "Or am I misremembering?"

"He never said he fell in love," Joanne clarified, cheeks flushing as she thought of Xavier. They'd done countless couple activities, yet here she was doubting. He knew her so deeply, better than most in some ways.

"Would someone improve a woman's business like that without love?" Nevaeh challenged, head cocked. "I think not. You love him, he loves you. I hear wedding bells!" She hummed the bridal march teasingly.

Courtney dabbed pizza grease from her fingers. "Your story is just so cute—enemies to lovers. She's a businesswoman, he fell in love, together they built an empire!" She clapped dramatically above her head. Joanne only grunted in response. "Come on; it's adorable you getting close to the 'enemy.'"

"She got a man from our rival town. Who knew?" Nevaeh cackled with Courtney, pulling faces and voices. Joanne hid behind her hands, fighting laughter at their antics.

"The only rivalry we have with Peachwood is football," she insisted around another pizza bite. "Otherwise, the towns get along fine."

New customers filtered in, but the girls paid them no mind, continuing their lively chatter without a care. An audience never stopped them from enjoying themselves to the fullest.

"There's always been a general rivalry," Brandi insisted, grabbing her third slice. "Haven't you heard Rochelle talk about it? It's a big deal." She took a hearty bite, patting her stomach. "I mean, no one's getting into fistfights, but since our towns are similar there's always been some healthy competition over who's better." Another bite, more pensive chewing. "At least with the older folks. *We* don't care much unless it's football." She wiped greasy fingers absently on a napkin. "You were on their side for that game, remember? Your tent was with the Peachwood crowd."

Nevaeh gasped dramatically before Joanne could object. Joanne rolled her eyes but allowed her to continue. "That's a sign we'll lose you faster than we thought!" She grasped Joanne's hand tightly. "Has Xavier mentioned you moving in already? That's an hour away! What about our lunch dates? Book club?"

Joanne winced, trying to tug her hand back. "Ow, too tight!" She pleaded at the giggling Courtney. "A little help here?" But Courtney just sipped her soda with no intention of intervening.

"But really, if you marry Xavier, you can't stay here, can you?" Brandi asked sadly, shoulders slumping.

Joanne flushed, fanning herself rapidly. "Hey now, I was joking about marrying him!"

"But isn't that what you want?" Courtney beamed knowingly. "You seem so in love, Jo."

Their expectant gazes made Joanne tingle and fidget. While she and Xavier weren't officially together, in her heart, it felt real. He'd been even more attentive and doting since their first date. She'd only moved back home in January because of him - with Xavier running Roasted Beans, she had peace of mind. Though initially resistant, she now gave him free rein with changes, each one bringing more delighted customers. He knew these people, their tastes, and passions.

His dedication proved his feelings to Joanne beyond doubt. Xavier didn't just care for her - he cared for all she held dear. When they talked now, goodbyes got harder every time, the space between meetings dragging endlessly. She found herself counting down the minutes until they'd reunite. Admitting her love without labels still frightened Joanne, but she could no longer deny the truth.

She giggled softly, picturing his perfect smile. "Okay, yes, I do love him, but I don't know..."

Courtney shushed her excitedly. "You love him, okay? Leave it at that. It's not too fast or too early - sometimes you just know. And that's what's happening with you two." She clapped giddily by her cheek.

Brandi nodded in agreement as more customers filed in, lining up at the counter. "Love at first sight is real, so of course falling for each other after seven months makes total sense." She leaned in conspiratorially as patrons found seats, chattering amongst themselves. "You are his girlfriend, whether he's said so or not. And he..."

"Is your man!" Nevaeh finished with a wink. Joanne rolled her eyes but couldn't help smiling. "Stop overthinking everything. You need to embrace these feelings, like we did with our boos. Just enjoy Xavier; it's okay to gush over him!"

Joanne laughed, giving in. "Okay, fine, I love him!" She joined their gleeful squealing, ignoring the few looks it drew. "Admitting it felt so good!" She clapped rapidly, her heart swelling with joy. "Imagine us moving in together!"

"But you'd be a whole hour away!" Courtney wailed dramatically. "I don't want you to go, Jo!" The girls begged her not to abandon them.

Joanne smiled, touched by their plea. "Guys, I won't be that far. Xavier's in the country between our towns—that's like a thirty-minute drive max. I'll visit all the time, or he can move here. We'll figure it out."

Courtney still pouted. "Well, as long as you're happy, I guess we should be, too. Just think—if Xavier proposed, three of us would be engaged!" She flashed her ring, Nevaeh following suit. Brandi and Joanne hooted and hollered.

As the conversation meandered, Joanne's mind lingered on her imagined future with Xavier — living together and having a family. Where would their children go to school? Being between towns gave them options. She was getting ahead of herself, but the daydreams felt so real, so right. Did Xavier feel the same way? He treated her like a queen, but did he truly love her, too? Either way, Joanne had never felt so adored.

CHAPTER TWENTY

ednesdays and Fridays were when Xavier shined brightest. He'd rise early to work out, entering the shop with infectious enthusiasm. Customers and staff alike noticed his peppy attitude on those days, realizing the source. While good-natured teasing ensued, Xavier didn't mind - as long as he got to see her.

"I got it," he said, retying his apron by her desk. Joanne typed away as he watched admiringly. "We add honey vanilla iced coffees for spring. And let customers add more toppings - candies, sprinkles, everything." He leaned forward, fingertips grazing her desk. "You see how crazy it gets with the festival coming? When spring really hits, we'll have twice the customers. More variety is key."

He sat back smugly, leg crossed. Today Joanne wore a sharp purple pantsuit and heels, makeup and hair done up. She always dressed so nicely for her visits, letting him handle things up front. He loved their balanced dynamic.

"I like the floral theme since spring is all about flowers. What other flower flavors could we offer?" Joanne clicked her pen, leaning back thoughtfully. The chair creaked under her movement. "Honey vanilla we already have..." She rolled closer. "What if we created our own special flavor?"

Xavier grinned, loving her willingness to explore new things. "That's a great idea. We could try another spring flower and make it our own." His heart quickened as her fingers flew across the keys. "Looking up options?" He leaned over her shoulder eagerly.

"Yes!" she sang. "Jasmine sounds really nice. I've had jasmine tea but not coffee. Do you think that could work?" Her dazzling smile sent his pulse racing faster.

Xavier drank in her beautiful face before answering. "There are Jasmine coffee beans used to make incredible Jasmine coffee. I've had some in my time. It's sophisticated yet appealing. I think our customers would love it on the menu. Should we start ordering the beans?" Though he spoke of work, his mind was far away, lost in her. Joanne turned him into a besotted fool.

Joanne opened a document, typing out "Jasmine Coffee" then tidying a loose hair. "Let's get a few more options first before jumping ahead," she said. "But I can see this being perfect for April." She spun playfully in her chair.

Laughing, Xavier stopped her spin to face him. Her excitement made his heart soar. "I've got plenty more spring coffee ideas," he purred, leaning close.

Joanne pressed a finger to his lips, though nearly nose-to-nose. "Tell me later when you're done managing the shop. It sounds pretty chaotic out there." She grimaced at the bustling noise beyond. The festival had the whole town ravenous. Their pastries were a roaring success, cookies and tarts flying off shelves. Xavier took pride in giving people what they craved.

"I'm sure it's fine, but I'll check for you." He blew a kiss and retreated, her sweet giggles music to him. But Joanne called him back - something about her tone gave him pause. "What is it?" he asked, returning to the chairs.

She fidgeted, clearly working up to something big. Xavier waited, intrigued. "Everything okay, Ms. Richards?"

Joanne tapped her pen on the desk. "We've gotten to know each other pretty well, haven't we?"

Eager for any extra time with her, Xavier chuckled. "Very well, working so close together." He sat, heart lifting at her soft expression. "I wish I could know you even better, but you're back in Sweetgum. Unless you moved here..." He trailed off hopefully.

Joanne sighed. "Sweetgum is home, I can't see myself leaving." She clicked her pen faster. "Unless it was for something really important."

Xavier's heart quickened at the look in her eye. "Something or someone?" he asked hopefully, barely breathing as he awaited her answer. If Joanne agreed to move in, he might actually backflip in joy - prior injury be damned.

Joanne drummed her fingers on the desk, smirking for a moment before her expression grew serious. "You and I...we're a thing, right?"

Xavier blinked in surprise. "What do you mean 'a thing'?"

"You know what I mean, don't play dumb," she huffed, leaning away wearily.

"I'm not playing, I just want to be sure..." Xavier settled back into the seat. "Are you asking if we're a couple?"

Joanne gave a short nod, features softening.

Xavier laughed in relief. "Of course we are! Did you think I was just taking you on dates and kissing you for fun?" He leaned forward eagerly. "I thought it was clear we were together. My girl-friend." Saying the words thrilled him.

"Well you never actually called me that, so how should I know?" Joanne avoided his gaze as her wall rose slightly. "Lots of people get involved without it being serious."

"You're right, I'm sorry." Xavier held up his hands, chastened. "I shouldn't have assumed. In this day and age you have every right to ask where we stand." He thumped his chest somberly. "Yes, I see you as my significant other. Do you feel the same about me?"

Joanne's shoulders relaxed as she smiled. "I do. I'm glad we're on the same page now."

Xavier grinned. "This is the longest relationship I've had, now that you mention it." Her intimate questions didn't faze him. "What else do you want to know?"

Joanne sipped her water thoughtfully. "Why so few relationships before? And why stay single so long?" She eyed him curiously. "I'm the only woman you've looked at since college, you said."

Xavier laughed at her analysis. "Who says I haven't been looking?" he teased.

"But really," Joanne pressed sweetly. "Tell me about your past love life. I want to know everything about you."

Xavier's grin softened. Her interest and trust meant the world. "All right, what do you want to know?" He settled in, ready to share it all.

Joanne collected herself, taking a moment to adjust her laptop's mouse pad before leaning in with curiosity. "You told me specifically, but that's not what we're talking about," she began, her tone measured. "Why have you stayed single, and why don't you date frequently? Are you picky?"

Xavier contemplated her question. "It's not really that. It's just..." He paused, searching for the right words. "Dating can be a bit tricky."

"Because sometimes you get screwed over?" Joanne offered with a knowing look. "If you're looking for that forever person, you have to explore. I'd be lying if I said I've been actively searching for someone myself, but my main problem is being busy."

Xavier chuckled at her response. "And now, the person you're with is busy with you."

Joanne rolled her eyes playfully. "I want to hear your real reason for being single. I promise I'll stop putting words in your mouth."

Xavier brought his hand up to his neck, massaging it gently as he thought. He then shrugged, as if trying to convey the complexity of his feelings. "I don't know. I guess I just haven't found the right person. Maybe I have a rare type? It's a lot of things, really. Overall, I've been busy too." He looked at Joanne, who appeared slightly puzzled. "Joanne?"

"You haven't met the right person?" Joanne asked for clarification.

Xavier realized he should have chosen his words more carefully. "No, I—"

Suddenly, there was a loud interruption from outside. "Mr. Evans? We're stretched thin out there, and a batch of cookies just got charred! Sir, can you come help? It's driving everyone crazy!" a frantic employee urgently called out.

Xavier felt a pang of frustration as he reluctantly rose from his seat. Before leaving, he turned to face Joanne.

Her phone rang, and she answered it promptly, her tall heels clicking on the carpet as she moved toward the window. "Roasted Beans Coffee Spot, how may I help you?" she greeted the caller.

Xavier hesitated, torn between going to help and saying a proper goodbye to Joanne. He decided to make a quick exit. Rushing to her desk, he leaned in and planted a kiss on her cheek. Joanne responded with a faint smile, but her expression hinted that he might have made a misstep. Xavier contemplated staying longer, but the barista's call for help beckoned him outside, and he hurried away.

"You take care, okay?" Xavier waved at the last employee while wiping the counter. He heard the doorbell ring and took a deep breath. Night had crept up on him unexpectedly. It felt like just a little while ago that he and Joanne had been talking. But the entire day had slipped by before they could reconnect. Joanne often stayed back late, so now seemed like the best time to explain himself.

He tossed the dirty wipe into a bin by the coffee makers and made his way to Joanne's office. "Joanne?" He walked with a sense of purpose, gathering his thoughts along the way. Upon reaching Joanne's office door, he found it locked. "Joanne?" Xavier twisted the doorknob and then stepped back. "Huh..." She must have left. He wandered around aimlessly, wondering what it meant. They always locked up together when she visited. What made tonight different? Had he unintentionally offended her?

Xavier felt a sense of defeat. Perhaps he was overthinking things. Joanne probably just needed an early start on her drive home. It was a long commute for her. "Right," he told himself. That had to be it.

Without further delay, Xavier retrieved his keys and jingled them all the way to the front. After ensuring every light was off and the shop was spotless, he locked up alone, as he had gotten used to doing, and made his way to his waiting vehicle.

Sitting alone in the driver's seat, he couldn't help but replay their recent conversation in his mind. "I'm overthinking it," he muttered. He briefly considered sending a text but decided against it. He didn't want to come across as desperate. Besides, something like this should be addressed in person. Whatever 'this' was. "Maybe it's just a misunderstanding," he said to himself.

With that, he sighed and revved the engine. Driving home in silence sounded like a good idea at this point.

CHAPTER TWENTY-ONE

Fifty messages filled Joanne's phone, but she hadn't even glanced at them. It hurt too much to do so.

She gripped the steering wheel, her teeth piercing her lower lip. Last Friday, she had deliberately rearranged her schedule to avoid crossing paths with Xavier. No matter how hard he tried to make plans, she came up with excuses to keep them apart. Why had she been so foolish?

The radio played a weather report, describing the clear skies of another spring day. Oh, how Joanne wished her own heart was as clear. She fought back tears, not wanting to appear weak. Deep down, she knew she should have seen this coming. Xavier would never see someone with as much emotional baggage as "the one." During his first few months working for her, she had made his life a living hell. Not to mention the ugly past she had shared. No man wanted a broken woman, and the same went for women with broken men. Yes, they had shared plenty of fun moments, and he had even referred to them as a couple, but it was clear what he meant. He hadn't found the right person. If it had been her, he would have said so without hesitation. The feelings were not mutual.

Tears welled in her eyes, and she let out a silent sob. She was about fifteen minutes away from her destination. She could see rows of trees whizzing by in her peripheral view as she sped down the highway. Normally, Wednesdays were a highlight of her week, but today was different. The same went for last Friday. Facing Xavier was embarrassing. Why had she let herself believe that he felt the same way? She shouldn't have fallen so hard or so fast. Baring her soul to him? What had she been thinking? Since the incident last Wednesday, she couldn't stop replaying it in her mind. Whenever her friends brought him up, she would say nothing in response. They seemed to have picked up on something happening, and Joanne would talk about it, but the shame was too much.

Finally, she parked along the sidewalk beside her newest branch. Through the window, she watched as customers filed in. All day long, they had a steady stream of patrons. She considered it a blessing, but she couldn't muster a smile. Joanne scolded herself inwardly, urging herself not to let one man ruin what was great in her life. She patted her cheeks and wiped her eyes. After dabbing them dry, her dismal mood brightened. It still irked her how upset she had gotten, but she knew work had to be done.

Joanne clamped her car shut and marched towards the entrance, clutching her handbag as she swung the door open. She made a beeline for the back of the building, hoping that Xavier would be in his office. She had checked his schedule earlier; he had a video call meeting with some suppliers. If she stayed at her desk and kept her door locked, she could limit their interactions. She preferred zero interactions, but that wasn't possible.

The soft carpet felt comforting under her feet as she reached her office door. She glanced at Xavier's door as she passed by. It was closed, and she silently thanked whatever forces were at play that he had shut it. Seeing him, even if it were just a glimpse through a crack, would only disrupt her focus. There were emails waiting for her response and phone calls to be made. Joanne needed to stay focused. No matter how much thinking about Xavier ached her heart, she had to press on.

With her keys jingling, she unlocked her office door and swung it open. She worked on autopilot, switching on the lights and heading to her desk, her eyes focused on the keys she dropped into her handbag. As her chunky heels tapped against the carpet, she sensed the presence of someone in her office.

"Good morning, Ms. Richards."

"What the—" Joanne jumped, clutching her bag tightly. Her heart raced as she realized that Xavier was there. He spun her chair left and right, sitting behind her large desk. His usual playfulness was absent, and his strong arms were folded across his chest. Panic swelled within her. It was him, the one she had been avoiding. Everything about him was as perfect as she remembered, and it infuriated her. "Who do you think you are, sneaking into my office like this? How did you get in without a key?" A numbing sickness churned in her stomach. "Xavier, this is creepy. How did you enter?"

"There's a spare key to your office in mine. You told me about it in case of emergencies," he said as he rolled the chair back and stood up. "Joanne," his voice carried a hint of hurt. His small frown revealed confusion and frustration. "What's gotten into you? Everything was going great. We went out on dates, texted all night, talked when we met, and now you won't even look at me?" He spread his arms open. "What happened? We're both adults. You can't just sideline me without explanation."

Joanne wanted to yell, scream, and shout, but Xavier's words rang true. She was a grown-up failing to communicate, and the "silent treatment" was often used by teenagers, not someone like her. This pain was making her feel repulsive, and she had to put an end to it. "Look," she couldn't bring herself to look at him, instead focusing on a small dolphin knick-knack on her desk. "I know we've had our fun, and we've worked really well together, but it's obvious to me that whatever this is can't continue." Her throat ached with each word, but she had to say it. Being so close to someone she loved who didn't feel the same was excruciating, and she couldn't continue to suffer like this. "So we need to go back to being just boss and manager, okay?" She kept her eyes fixed on the translucent dolphin.

There was silence. The man who usually had so much to say was speechless.

Joanne could almost hear his heart rate pick up, but she resisted the urge to lock eyes with him. His face would only make the situation more painful.

"Where is this coming from?" he finally breathed out, his voice close to her forehead.

When Xavier's soft, warm hands held her face, Joanne almost cracked. Her eyes filled with tears, but she refused to let them fall. Instead, she stepped away from his touch. At last, Joanne pointed to his chest. "You tell me, Xavier," she said, dropping her finger as she saw his raised brows reflecting complete bewilderment. "You tell me why you'd spend so much time with someone you didn't think was right. Why you'd treat them like a queen and whisper sweet words that helped them sleep at night. Why you'd hold them like they were the only one you cared about just to say they weren't what you wanted. Why you'd..." She whimpered, feeling like a baby. It was embarrassing. Tears again in front of Xavier. He had gone from lost to worried. Joanne watched as he stretched out a hand, which she swatted away. "Why you'd lead me on like that. Make me fall in love with you when you saw me as just another girl to break up with later." The shame was too much, and Joanne buried her face in her hands, crying.

Tenderly, Xavier placed a hand on her shoulder. "Joanne, what are you saying?" There was something in his voice that bothered her. Was that laughter? He seemed happy, but why? Was her agony entertaining to him? Her fury surged, almost blinding her, but Joanne contained it. She slipped out of his touch and turned her back on him. Xavier Evans would mock her no longer.

As she took her second step toward the door, he grabbed her hand. "Wait," he said, laughing.

"What about this is funny to you, huh?" Joanne challenged him. "Is it because you got the stone-cold owner to fall for your charm? Is that what's so hilarious?" She scrunched her nose in annoyance, ready to tell him off. "If that's it, then I want you to know that you are the definition of scum, Xavier. How dare you play with a woman like—"

He placed a finger to her lips, silencing her. "Joanne," he said softly. "Listen. You didn't let me finish last week." He held both her shoulders and looked into her eyes with patience and understanding. "I hadn't dated since college until I met you because you're the right one. I realized that you misinterpreted my words, but I never got the chance to explain because you started avoiding me. Did you even read my texts? I said this in at least four of them, but you stopped interacting." He pinched both her hands between his fingers. "That's what I've been trying to tell you. You're the one, Joanne. And for as long as you'll have me, I'll keep letting you take charge while I push you out of your comfort zone." He ended with a devilish wink and a warm smile.

All of Joanne's fears and doubts vanished. The knots in her stomach unraveled, and the ice around her heart melted. "Xavier," she thought of him with a halo over his head, and as if on cue, he smiled, radiating warmth. "I love you," she whispered, her heart swelling with happiness.

Xavier chuckled softly. "I love you too, Jo. But we need to communicate."

"I know. I'm so sorry," she confessed, rubbing her cheek against his shoulder and then pulling back to look into his eyes. "I just... I have a lot of pride," she admitted, her face flushed. "I swear I'm not usually that immature."

The kind-hearted man nodded understandingly. "I know you aren't. You were just really hurt, but it's okay now. You know how I truly feel," he nuzzled her affectionately, and a smile spread across his face as their foreheads touched.

Without hesitation, Joanne puckered her lips and pressed them to his. Their kiss was tender and full of affection, and in each other's embrace, Joanne found peace.

CHAPTER TWENTY-TWO

"The special effects in this movie are horrible," Joanne commented as she stirred her noodles in the Styrofoam cup. She sat cross-legged on Xavier's couch on a Friday night in April. The sliding doors of the kitchen were wide open, letting in the cool spring breeze. Xavier's place was perfect for spring sleepovers.

Xavier, wrapping thick bands of noodles around his chopsticks, glanced at the giant lizard on the screen, humming in thought. "It could be worse. This film is from the nineties. I think they did a decent job," he said, his voice muffled as he chewed his food. Their altercation two weeks ago had actually strengthened their relationship. Following that, they had collaborated on various projects to improve all the Roasted Beans branches, which had taken effect last week. Xavier had even accompanied her to Sweetgum to implement them, where he had met her friends and family. They were nice people. The special Spring karaoke event had been a hit, as had their new coffee offerings. Roasted Beans patrons in both towns loved what they offered, and sales were through the roof. In honor of their success, he and Joanne had given themselves a well-deserved break.

Xavier had recently purchased another commercial property in Peachwood, but he wasn't sure what to do with it yet. Joanne mainly managed her work from home, but next week, they'd both be back in business. Xavier found himself liking it in Sweetgum; the people there were friendly.

"If this were a sixties movie, then yeah, it'd be impressive, but the nineties should have been more progressive. Yikes," Joanne continued to criticize Xavier's chosen film. She ate her food and licked her lips. The center table was littered with snacks they had bought from the grocery store. When this film ended, they planned to watch another. Joanne had already picked a classic from her childhood. "But I do see the charm of this movie," she added with an amused expression. He could see her lips threatening to stretch into a grin. "Bad movies can be good because they're so bad."

Xavier had a good laugh. Whenever Joanne slept over, he never wanted to sleep. Closing his eyes in the presence of perfection felt criminal. He didn't want to waste her time. Not when she wouldn't be around forever. But that could all change. He finished his noodles, put down the cup, and wrapped an arm around his girl-friend. Joanne leaned in, playing with her food. She was dressed in a tank top and shorts as pajamas, exposing her skin to him. He had chosen a T-shirt and boxer shorts to sleep in. "I'm glad you see the upside to bad movies," he said, kissing her cheek. "They're fun to laugh at."

"They sure are," Joanne agreed as she continued to enjoy her food.

He gave her some time to finish before he spoke again. "So... it's been a while since we've met and a while since we've started dating," he began slowly. "We've had our ups and downs, but I think that in the past few weeks, we've found a sweet spot to just enjoy each other," he said, squeezing her close. "Am I right?"

She wiped her lips with a napkin. "Yes, you are," Joanne replied, her nose almost touching his. "Things are going pretty nicely. We have our business, our date days, we travel between towns, and sleep over when we can," she listed with a smug tone, looking very pleased. "I don't think anything can mess us up now," but her face then dropped. "Unless you have some other major secret to drop on me."

Xavier shook his head. "No, no. Of course not," he assured her. "I wouldn't do that to you. We're open and honest with each other, remember?" He kissed her cheek, and that seemed to calm her down. "The reason I started saying all this is because," he paused, searching for the right words. "I've loved spending time with you. Anyone else might get tired of someone they work so closely with, but it hasn't been that way with you for me. I just can't get enough of Joanne Richards, and I'm not ashamed to admit it," he said, feeling a sense of accomplishment when she shyly rubbed her shoulder.

"If I could make a wish right now, it would be to spend even more time with you. To live with you so we won't have to part as often."

Joanne blinked a few times. "What are you saying?" her lips stretched into a genuine grin.

Xavier shrugged. "Would you want to maybe... move in with me?"

Joanne gasped and froze, mouth hanging open.

He wasn't sure what to think. He had thought he had eased her into it, but now she looked surprised. "Too soon? I just thought it's been eight months, so why not?" he laughed nervously, awaiting her reply.

"Xavier," Joanne sat up, her face lit up with elation. "That's an amazing idea! Yes. Why not? Of course, I want to move in with you," she embraced him tightly, nearly sliding into his lap.

Phew. He knew she'd say yes, but the brief pause had shocked him. Sometimes, Joanne could be unpredictable, even to someone who knew her well. "So you'll move in? It's not too far from home?"

"At this point, you're my home, so it's okay," she said, planting a sloppy kiss on his cheek. "But we're switching sides on the bed. If that's okay with you," she teased as she cupped his left cheek.

"Honestly," Xavier replied, pulling her legs onto his lap, "I'd make whatever changes you desire as long as it moves you in faster." He ensured she was comfortable sitting on his thighs before they began discussing their future – where Joanne would put her stuff and what renovations could be made. The two were on the same wavelength in every sense, but when contrasting ideas were mentioned, they listened and gave their opinions. All the while, Xavier's cheap horror movie played in the background, no longer the center of their attention with this new exciting arrangement on the horizon.

EPILOGUE

$\mathcal{A}$ unanimous groan filled the living room as an obvious foul was overlooked by the referee. Xavier leaped from his seat to protest, with Sean, Justin, and Chris backing him up, wildly gesturing at Sean's TV. Their team was only a point behind, and the referee wasn't doing them any favors. Each man had donned blue and white jerseys to match their favorite players. Popcorn, sodas, and licorice littered Sean's central table. Some snacks had found their way onto the carpet, but none of them cared. When the game was in progress, it had them all hooked.

Brandi had just returned from the living room with an empty tray. "They're like toddlers watching that popular kids' show, completely immersed," she remarked, setting the dish down near where Nevaeh was washing dishes. While their partners went berserk in the living room, the four friends—plus Tia—caught up in the kitchen. They had already devoured four family-sized servings of chips. The kitchen table was a haven of junk food. Courtney sat at it with Joanne, both of them stuffing their faces with cheese balls, while Brandi and Nevaeh took care of the cleanup. Tia sat on the counter, swinging her legs while holding a packet of chocolate. Just like their zealous male companions, the ladies were decked out in jerseys, too. "Game Night" was a serious event.

"I'm just waiting for Xavier to jump through the screen," Courtney remarked as she peeked into the living room. She smiled and turned to Joanne, who rolled her eyes. "That man is serious about his football. Be careful, or he may marry the game before he marries you."

Laughter erupted from her friends, and Joanne dramatically flipped her hair. "Oh, please. If I walked in there right now, he'd forget all about that washed-up team," she declared, popping two cheese balls into her mouth. "Feels like it's been forever since we all hung out." She glanced at Nevaeh, who had just finished drying her hands. Brandi leaned beside Tia near the counter. "You mentioned you had an announcement, right?"

Nevaeh's lip corners curled mischievously, and that was quite an accomplishment given her already well-established history of mischief. Many instances of Nevaeh's troublesome ways came to Joanne's mind. The girl was always up to something. "Indeed, I do," she said, tucking her long braids behind her ears. "But I'll spill the beans right after I make a quick bathroom trip. Girls, you are going to flip when I share the news." She began to skip away but returned with an extended finger, pointing at Tia. "Tia, don't spill the beans. They can't know until I spill them, so keep those little lips sealed," she pinched the child's mouth, prompting giggles. After briefly tickling her, Nevaeh finally skipped away to the bathroom.

Joanne observed Tia with a playful smirk. "Hmm, I wonder what it could be," she mused, leaning back and wiping cheese dust off her fingers, some of which fell into her half-eaten packet. As they conversed, the men remained standing, yelling at the screen and cheering when good plays were executed.

"You'll never guess. That's for sure," Tia replied with a giggle, her finger playfully pressed against her lips. Nevaeh had styled Tia's hair into an adorable twist-out, complete with a butterfly clip on the left.

Arching an eyebrow, Joanne couldn't help but tease, "Why do I feel like you might end up telling us before she does? Control yourself, Tia. Don't burst open," she said in a lighthearted tone. Both Courtney and Brandi couldn't help but smile at the child's enthusiasm. They had heard countless stories about why Tia was "smarter" than most kids, and they were witnessing it firsthand. Her vocabulary and her contributions to their discussions spoke for themselves.

Tia playfully covered her mouth with both hands, earning laughter from Joanne and Courtney.

Brandi tapped her chin as if pondering, "Let me see, is Nevaeh going to come back here and tell us about a new pony she bought you?" She brought her face close to Tia's.

With a mischievous grin, Tia uncovered her mouth and replied, "Nope." She swung her short legs, displaying a knowing smile. "Even if you guess right, I won't tell you," she added before playfully sealing her lips with her fingers.

Courtney then chimed in, "Oh wait, are you guys moving across the state?" Her eyes widened, and a hint of sadness crossed her expression. "Don't move, Tia. I'll miss you."

Tia leaned on the counter and stopped kicking her legs. She looked poised as she asked, "What about Nevaeh? Wouldn't you miss your best friend more, Courtney?"

Joanne waved her hand dismissively. "Nevaeh might be Courtney's friend, but I'm her best friend, okay? And I think I speak for all of us when I say we like you more," she teased. "I'm kidding." Despite their frequent disagreements, Nevaeh held a special place in Joanne's heart. If she were to move away, Joanne would feel a significant loss. Joanne already lived thirty minutes away, but that didn't deter them from spending time together. Thanks to her business, Joanne and Xavier saw the girls often. Living hundreds of miles away was a whole different story from living across town. She bit her thumb playfully. "That's not what's happening, right, Tia? You can at least confirm that."

Tia raised her shoulders and made gestures that clearly communicated 'I don't know.' "It could be anything. We could be getting a new dog, a new cat, a new goat..."

"I like how all your suggestions involve pets," Courtney chuckled as she grabbed a handful of cheese puffs from her bag. "If Nevaeh was moving, she'd be much sadder, guys. She wouldn't call moving away from us an exciting announcement."

Joanne nodded in agreement. "Sounds like you're trying to convince yourself more than anyone here. But I do agree with you. Hmm... she's been looking extra gorgeous these days, though. Like she has a glow."

Brandi placed a hand behind Tia's back, gently stroking the small girl and wrapping her arms around her. "She's always glowing, but you have a point. Lately, it's like she's on a different level. Do you think—oh wait, is she pregnant?" she gasped.

The room fell into silence.

Tia once again mimed zipping her lips shut. "Maybe. Maybe not. Your guess is as good as mine," she replied with a coy smile. "Or maybe she's just extra happy about our new dog."

Joanne chuckled as she approached Tia and Brandi. "Okay, that's enough. Your uncle and Nevaeh have got to get you a puppy," she said with a playful tone. She wiped her fingers clean and twisted the empty portion of her bag. Getting up, she shuffled over to Tia and Brandi. She playfully tapped Tia's chin and teased, "But imagine if she is pregnant. That would be the first baby of our group. Apart from Tia, of course," she grinned at the child. "Who wants to take turns looking after Baby Nev?" She playfully envisioned an energetic little girl with Nevaeh's smile and energy. "Oh goodness. Never mind. You two can discuss that amongst yourselves. I'd rather stay clear of anything like that." The hearty laughter from her friends confirmed she was kidding.

Brandi shook her head, offering her own speculation. "It was just a guess. I don't know what's really happening. I'd say she's engaged, but she already is. Oh! Maybe the wedding is closer than we think. How about that?"

Joanne beamed at the idea. "It could be that," she said, turning to Courtney. "What do you think? Ready to be her maid of honor?" She playfully danced with a shimmy of her shoulders.

Courtney pretended to be taken aback. "Wouldn't that go to Brandi?" She looked around the room as the guys cheered and jumped around while engrossed in the football game. "Nev was Brand's maid of honor. It's how she met Sean and little Tia." She blew kisses toward the child.

Joanne grinned and nodded. "We're all taking turns, so next will be you." She noticed Nevaeh dancing her way into the room, albeit poorly, and smiled nonetheless. "Okay. Ready to make the big announcement?" The notion that Nevaeh might get married before Courtney was quite surprising, given Nevaeh's tendency to procrastinate despite the closeness of their engagements.

"Yes, I am," Nevaeh declared, flipping her braids around. With hands on her hips, she cleared her throat dramatically. "I am more than excited to inform all of you, my closest friends, that I..." She placed her hand on her lower stomach for emphasis. "Am expecting!"

Joanne's jaw dropped in shock, and Brandi let out a delighted squeal. Courtney clapped her hands together before rushing over to Nevaeh. Joanne started hopping up and down in excitement. "Nevaeh, that's amazing! Congratulations!" she exclaimed, dashing over to hug both Nevaeh and Courtney. Brandi quickly joined the group, and they all bounced around joyfully, nearly toppling over in their enthusiasm. Soon, a tiny body emerged to share in their jubilation, and the girls opened themselves up to Tia, fitting her into the middle.

"I'm going to be a big sister!" Tia announced with a spin before hugging Nevaeh. "He's going to be a boy, and we'll name him Tio!"

The four friends laughed heartily at Tia's adorable imagination. "We'll see about that, okay, T?" Nevaeh patted Tia's head lovingly. "I'm so excited. It's been hard keeping this in. I wanted to yell it from the rooftops the second I found out, but what better occasion to share this than with all of my favorite girls around me?" She wrapped her arms around Courtney and Brandi, holding them all tightly.

Joanne couldn't contain her happiness, and she wiped away a few stray tears that had slipped from her eyes. "I'm so happy for you. Does Sean know? Wait, of course he does if Tia knows," she said, her voice filled with joy. "We should tell the rest of the guys now, if you're open to sharing." She was buzzing with excitement at the thought of becoming an aunt. How precious it would be!

Nevaeh snapped her fingers in agreement and hurried to the living room. "Boys, I just told the girls something incredible!" she exclaimed, jumping in front of the screen.

"Wait, you told them?" Sean asked as he got up, a soda can in hand. He moved to Nevaeh's side, wrapping an arm around her lower waist.

Now, the living room was filled to capacity. Joanne found Xavier and squeezed herself between his arm and body. He seemed intrigued by what Nevaeh would say, but he first looked to Joanne for a hint.

She shook her head, signaling him to listen. Her friends each held their respective partners, all of whom had risen from their seats. Nevaeh had the floor, and everyone was listening. The game served as background noise to "take two" of Nevaeh's announcement.

With excitement, Nevaeh clapped her hands before shouting, "I'm pregnant!"

"Wow!" A stream of congratulations and applause filled the room. The guys surrounded Sean, patting his back in pride. They exchanged several hugs with the beaming Nevaeh to show their support, and every face bore a smile. It was impossible not to grin with delight.

"Did you tell them the other part?" Sean asked with both arms around his girl. Tia held onto his leg while Nevaeh rubbed her cheek against his.

"Oh no, I forgot," Nevaeh admitted with a sheepish grin as she gathered her hands again. "Due to this pregnancy, Sean and I would like to get married in five weeks," she held up five fingers. "We don't want to put it off any longer. So, everyone, get your best outfits and clean up. The wedding is on in less than two months!" She pumped her happy fists in the air, and in response, the room erupted in more applause.

"Wow," Xavier said, squeezing Joanne close. "My first big game night turned into something huge," he added, looking over the moon. "It's like I'm part of the family."

"You are," Joanne snuggled into his chest, her heart filled with warmth and joy. Her friends blocked the TV, talking animatedly about babies and weddings. Nevaeh tried to calm them down by focusing on the wedding preparations. They needed to tackle one thing at a time, as Nevaeh wisely put it. "And I'm so glad to have you," Joanne said, basking in the kiss Xavier planted on her forehead. In the end, she and her friends had found amazing guys to settle down with, and each seemed comfortable and deeply in love with their chosen partners. Joanne looked at Xavier and couldn't help but think that, to her, he was certainly the best one.

AUTHOR'S NOTE

Thank you so much for reading In Charge, the fifth book in the Sweetgum Meadows Romance series of stand-alone novels. I really hope you loved it! If you enjoyed this book, please consider leaving it a review so that others may also find it. Also, if you haven't read the first four books, yet, check them out today! Although these are stand-alone novels, the stories all intertwine and progress.

I look forward to introducing you to the other characters in this lovely, family-oriented town where each couple will find their happily ever after.

Would you like to receive bonus scenes and keep up with what's next with my upcoming books? Then, make sure you sign up for my mailing list on my website by visiting ImaniPrice.com.

To all my lovely readers,

Thank you for reading